The Dreamer Falls

Book 3 of The Secret of the Tirthas

Steve Griffin

Copyright © Steve Griffin 2016

Contents

For Sam

Prologue

The fire blazing in the hearth of the great, vault-like hall made little impression on the chilly air.

In the centre of the room four people, breaths misting, surrounded a colossal painting that had been laid down flat on the flagstone floor. The subject of the painting wore a full suit of polished armour, with a giant sword sheathed in a scabbard. Most people when they first saw the portrait usually thought it must be a man, but those who took the time to inspect it closer realised that it was in fact a woman. Albeit a masculine-looking woman, with long brown hair, a fine, angular face and dark, lustrous eyes.

The men standing around the portrait were an unusual group drawn from different quarters of the world – a young, bald Asian in casual western clothes; a distinguished, grey-haired man with glasses, wearing a tweed jacket; and a middle-aged Indian with a turban and a gold-fringed tunic.

The origins of the fourth figure, who was crouching down in front of the portrait, were more obscure. Dressed in a fur-trimmed purple robe and an extravagant headdress like a pharaoh, his elaborate clothes belied a shrunken, withered frame. His ancient face was pasty white, with thin pink lips that looked like they had been painted on. But despite his decrepit appearance his eyes, tiny and blue, blazed as he crawled forward on to the portrait, clutching a vial filled with red liquid in one hand.

'Mistress, here is the witchkin's blood that the Hoodoo priest, Paterson, gave to Lamya...' he said in a soft, rasping voice.

'He told me Lizzie's blood would probably have done just as well as Caroline's,' said the man in the tweed jacket in a refined English accent to the Indian. But the Indian barely acknowledged him, his eyes intent on the painting.

Then, with surprising swiftness, the ancient figure crawling on the painting struck the vial down and it smashed, spilling its dark contents over the pale face of the portrait.

'Our Lady...' he said, his eyes widening and his mouth opening to reveal long brown canines. He hissed like a violent cat as the air began to shimmer and cackle, as something, *someone*, a tall, handsome woman, *the woman in the portrait*, suddenly appeared out of nothing at the far end of the picture.

'Lady Eva,' said the ancient being, bowing his head. '*Pisaca...*'

Chapter 1: The Buddha's Tooth

The girl with the ponytail was walking beside the garden brook with a tall, bald old man dressed in an orange robe. A small dog with golden fur bounced alongside them, snapping at butterflies and a green emperor dragonfly that swerved assuredly up and down the babbling stream.

'...so you're saying The Book of Life is supposed to have been dictated to this ancient...*mystic*... by some kind of *immortal?*' said the girl, Lizzie Jones.

'Yes,' replied the man, Xiao Xing. The Chinese monk had been translating the ancient book that Lizzie and her companions had recovered after the fight with Chen Yang and the monster dogs in the basement of Lady Blane's house.

'You've got to be kidding,' said Lizzie.

'That's what Ho Lung – the mystic who wrote it – says. He went up into the Hengduan mountains for a period of seventeen days and nights and experienced the most appalling weather. Rainstorms and lightning, searing heat, gales, hailstones the size of mice. He lived in a cave and was visited every night by the immortal, the dragon Lu Win. Lu exhaled a torrent of blazing words into his mind, his struggle was to write them all down before he forgot them.'

Lizzie laughed. 'I can't believe it,' she said.

'Yet you've battled with the woman Eva Blane, who turned into a monster, and the man Paterson who stopped time with a spell.'

'Well, when you put it like that...'

Lizzie was quiet for a moment, thinking. The straw-coloured dog flung himself into the stream, and began lapping up the water.

'Mr Tubs is hot,' said Xing.

'Supernatural beings,' said Lizzie. 'Existing on a different plane, alongside ours...'

'Alongside, through, on top of, underneath, it all depends on your point of view.'

'Yes, yes, only words, I get it. But you're saying they actually come *out* of the *Astral Plane* via the tirthas, and... and some of them terrorise and feed off *people* – like Eva, the Pisaca?'

'Yes. Some of them. And some of them do other things, like having children with normal people.'

'*What?*'

Suddenly Xing's face broke into a wide smile and he stopped, gazing through an opening past a small gnarly tree. Lizzie could see a bright dotted mosaic of a blue lizard in the rock garden beyond.

'The Rainbow Serpent Garden!' Xing exclaimed, before looking down at the bushes. 'I always told Evelyn those oakleaf hydrangeas would look lovely there.'

Lizzie smiled. 'You were saying...'

'What?'

'About some of those Astral beings having children with ordinary people...'

'Oh yes,' he said, as they resumed walking. 'I think Mr Paterson, the Hoodoo priest, wasn't from the tirthas – he died far too easily. Quite often these magical beings are tough to kill on Earth, because they need to be destroyed on their own Plane, or by special objects. And sometimes they're difficult to kill because they hide their souls in a phylactery.'

'What's a phylactery?'

'A special object used to protect the soul in the event of the body being killed,' said Xing. 'Once it's destroyed, the soul returns to the body, and the creature can be killed for good.

'I suspect Mr Paterson's mother or father might have been a being from the tirthas,' he continued. 'That would have given Paterson some power to do magic.'

Lizzie shook her head and laughed. 'But it's only a book, right?'

'Yes, only a book. But one that also describes how once there was a single stream of power, like an umbilical cord, linking the Astral Plane with Earth, and how ancient processes – magical processes, but also more mundane ones like plate tectonics – pulled that cord apart and dragged remnants of it across the planet.

'And those ancient remnants became the sacred places where early humans decided to worship, weaving stories about the mysterious creatures that visited them,' added Xing. 'Visited them *through the tirthas.*'

'And you think they're all still somehow connected and the centre of that 'umbilical cord' is *right here?* My great-uncle's garden?' Again Lizzie chuckled, this time barely containing a current of hysteria. She was imagining a giant cosmic baby, still joined to his... *what?*

The dragonfly, a bejewelled tube with black orbs for eyes, paused a short way in front of them.

'Be cautious,' said Xing. 'There's a spy in our midst.'

Lizzie watched the alien insect as it hovered perfectly, and wondered for a moment if Xing might actually *not* be joking.

'Who knows?' Xing continued, as the dragonfly suddenly powered up and over a nearby hedge. 'But what we do know is that the garden, unlike any of the other Remnants of the Severing, has many tirthas. And in the book, Ho Lung describes how the Nexus – let's assume it's our garden here – has special power. And how magical artefacts, created by people and infused with a potent blend of their long-lived worship and the power of the tirthas, can be used to harness that power for one's own ends. For avoiding summons to the Unknown Realms, for instance...'

'The Un...' began Lizzie.

'Oh!'

The person who cried out was neither the monk nor the girl, but rather a woman with brown hair in a checked shirt who appeared through a rose-spun arch which led back to the house, Rowan Cottage.

'Mum!' cried Lizzie.

'Lizzie!' said her mum, staring wide eyed at the venerable Chinese man in his saffron robe.

Lizzie couldn't believe it. Her mum was *meant* to be in Ludlow with her dreadful man-friend, Godwin Lennox. They'd only left an hour ago, which was why Lizzie had told Xing it was safe for him to come through the tirtha and discuss what he'd found in the Book – as well as take a more detailed look at the garden he'd helped Evelyn to create all those years ago.

'Mum...' she said more quietly, looking at the almost perfect 'O' of her mum's gaping mouth. She realised she was going to have to say something. 'This is...'

'Xing. Xiao Xing,' said the monk, stepping spritely forward and bringing up a hand. For a split second Lizzie thought she saw something in it, something dirty and yellow like a stone.

Rachel Jones raised a hand uncertainly and Xing shook it, before placing an arm around her shoulder and turning her gently back towards the house whose eaves peeped up above the nearby hedge. 'I'm one of Lizzie's friends, I'm helping her sort out all this pesky business of the tirthas,' he said.

'The tirthas?' said Rachel.

What?? screamed a voice in Lizzie's head. She noticed Tubs bounding off happily at the heels of Xing and her mum as they went through the rose arch.

'Yes,' said Xing, 'she's been having an amazing time, seeing all those far off places.'

'Really?' said Rachel.

'Of course, it hasn't all been fun and games. Not with some of the wicked creatures the tirthas keep coughing up!' said Xing, grinning and showing his teeth.

'What – what creatures...?'

As she followed silently along behind them, Lizzie wondered how much more her mind was going to be stretched before it finally snapped. *Not much more, that was for sure.* Over the past nine months she'd done everything humanly possible to keep her mum from knowing about the secret of the tirthas. And now here was her new friend Xiao Xing, giving it all away in a moment.

'Xing!' she said, but the monk didn't even acknowledge her as he continued towards the house with her mum.

'... a lot of friends who are helping her out,' said Xing.

'Friends? I didn't think she'd made any yet,' said her mum. 'Not that Thomas Bennett?'

'No, proper friends,' said Xing. 'The witches Ashlyn and Madeline from the village, and her Indian friends Pandu and Inspector Faruwallah. And now of course there's Caroline Day and her brother Miles, from Louisiana.'

'I have no idea what you're talking about,' said Rachel.

'Mum!' said Lizzie. 'I can explain...'

But her mum barely turned around to acknowledge her as Xing drew her on into the Sun Garden with its semi-circular hedge and bird table, the garden behind her great-uncle Eric's study.

'It will all make sense, one day,' said Xing, ignoring Lizzie's interruption. 'All you need to know is that she's in safe hands.'

'Oh,' said Rachel. 'Right.'

Xing released her shoulder and glanced back at the house. 'You can go inside now, Mrs Jones. Perhaps make yourself a cup of coffee. Forget all this for now.' Again he smiled.

Rachel looked up and down at his splendid robe, then into his calm, wrinkled face. She glanced at Lizzie and Mr Tubs who was staring up at her with his mouth open and pink tongue showing. Then she turned and without saying a word walked over and opened the door into the study. She stepped inside the house and in a moment was gone.

'What have you done?' Lizzie closed her eyes tight, her mind a storm of confusion.

'Don't worry,' said Xing. 'I'll explain on the way back to The Master of Nets Garden.'

With a final glance back through the study window, Lizzie followed the Chinese monk back towards the garden that contained the magical portal through which he had arrived. Mr Tubs trotted happily along behind them.

'How do we know she's not calling the police – or even worse, *Godwin* – right now?' said Lizzie, shuddering as she thought about how the relationship between her mum and the arrogant English businessman was developing so fast.

'Because of this.'

Xing stopped and held up the yellowish item that Lizzie had glimpsed in his hand. It was small, about the size of her thumb, with a faint patina.

'What is it, ivory?' she said.

'Close,' he replied. 'It's a tooth.'

'What kind of tooth?'

'A very special one. A tooth that belonged to a man who died a long time ago, Siddhartha Gautama.'

Lizzie felt a flash of irritation with the monk. With her brain still boiling from the appearance of her mum and all the things Xing had told her, the last thing she wanted was to have to guess what he was talking about.

'Siddhartha Gautama was a sage who lived in India two-and-a-half thousand years ago. You will probably know him better by another name – the Buddha.'

'That's one of the Buddha's *teeth?'* said Lizzie.

'Yes, we believe so. One of his teeth is kept in a temple in Kandy in Sri Lanka, but there are reported to be several more throughout the world. We have always held this one in our monastery on Mount Keung. It's not as well-known as the other relics of Gautama Buddha because we're so remote – but that doesn't mean for a moment it's not real.'

Lizzie stared in amazement at the object. It seemed so ordinary, ugly even. Could it really be that old? *And precious?*

Xing continued: 'I and the other monks on Keung have always known that the Tooth had some special properties, ever since Lao Guang used it to heal Sifu Lei's pneumonia. It's helped a few of us through some bad illnesses over the years. But it was when we had a visit from a very traumatised young man who'd been attacked and badly beaten by bandits that we realised its healing could extend to the soul.'

'How?' said Lizzie.

'It helped him to forget,' said the monk. 'Not forever, I think that would probably be impossible. But it took the pain away to a deeper part of his mind, enabling him to deal with the trauma of his situation at a... *manageable* rate.'

Lizzie thought for a moment. 'Do you mean it's just wiped Mum's memory?'

Xing nodded. 'She won't even remember me. Not unless you were to mention the incident to her again.'

'Wow...*wow!*' said Lizzie, still wondering whether to believe him.

'What's more, I think what I have here is also one of the Artefacts of Power mentioned in The Book of Life,' said Xing. 'It's been the object of merit-making amongst monks and the small number of outsiders who have visited us ever since the monastery and its gardens were founded, fifteen hundred years ago. It's a very special relic.'

'So how come you're carrying it around with you? Shouldn't it be kept safely in the monastery?'

'With all I've read, and everything you've told me, I've decided that it's best to keep it close to me. *Very* close. I think the Pisaca – and her helpers Paterson, Lamya, and Chen Yang – were all pursuing these objects with a plan. A wicked plan.'

15

'What kind of plan?'

'I think they wanted to use them to harness the power of the tirthas to prevent their summons to the Unknown Realms.'

'What are *they*?' said Lizzie. They walked through the entranceway to The Master of Nets garden and stopped in front of a miniature rocky wall at the edge of a pond. This was the *Barrier of Cloud* which concealed the tirtha, the one that could take Xing back to his monastery on Mount Keung in an instant.

'The Book of Life talks about a time when all the beings – the archetypes, gods, demons, fairies, dragons, and ghouls – who exist on the Astral Plane will be called away to a place of utter mystery. A place where they can no longer interact with the Earth and its people. That place it terms the *Unknown Realms*.'

'Sounds scary,' said Lizzie.

'Yes,' said Xing. 'Very scary. And that's why the few who still remain don't wish to go. And why they're doing all they can to avoid it.'

'So how can the Artefacts help?'

'I'm not sure. There's still more I need to translate, it's all written in a very archaic script. But we need to keep them under close guard, until we know.'

'Chen Yang escaped...' said Lizzie, thinking about Lamya's Chinese henchman who had fled from her and her friends in the basement of Eva's – the *Pisaca's* – house.

'Yes. And who knows if there are others in with them. Raj has said he's increased the guard around the

Lingam in Kashi, but I think you or Ashlyn should go back to Caroline and her brother in Louisiana and let them know. It sounds like Mr Paterson thought the native American doll Caroline was given by your great grandmother – *Sally Ally* – was one of the Artefacts. And if so, that needs to be kept safe too.'

Lizzie had a sensation of sinking, like a shadow coming down across her heart.

'We are safe, aren't we Xing?' she said. The last thing she felt she could take was more trouble from the tirthas. They had given her great joy – but immense pain, too.

'Yes, Lizzie,' said the Chinese man. 'We are safe – for now.'

He gave her a reassuring smile before he stepped over the Barrier of Cloud, leaving her staring at the dark hedge that a moment ago had been obscured by his orange robes.

Instinctively she knelt down and tugged Tubs close up against her.

Chapter 2: The Mask in the Border

'Have you heard about the Bennett's boy, Thomas?'

Godwin Lennox breezed into the Rowan Cottage kitchen where Lizzie and her mum were having cheese on toast for lunch. Mr Tubs was sat on his haunches beside Lizzie, hoping for a crust.

'No,' said Rachel, before catching the scowl on her daughter's face and saying in a quiet voice: 'Hope you don't mind, I gave him a spare key, in case we lose ours...'

'Little urchin's gone missing,' said Godwin.

'No!' said Rachel.

'Yes, last seen the day before yesterday. My friend Jim, the Assistant Chief Constable, told me. There's a search being organised right now.'

'No way!' said Lizzie, forgetting for a moment the flux of blinding fury mixed with utter despair she felt because her mum had given Godwin a key to their house.

'Could get quite serious,' said Godwin. 'Jack – from the Spar – has had a call from *The Mail*. Perhaps the village witches – Ashlyn Williams, Madeline Kendall and co. – are up to their old tricks again. A child sacrifice to make up for missing the solstice or something.'

'Don't be silly!' said Rachel, smiling. She thought for a moment then said: 'Do you remember that boy who was seen in the woods last winter?'

'The *Feral Child?*' said Godwin.

'Yes. They didn't ever find him, did they?'

'No. I reckon that might've been a bit of collective imagining and embellishing. My tenant – Burt Eames, the one who saw him in his barn – likes his cider.'

Lizzie bit her tongue – literally – and had to stop herself from *ouching*. If only she could tell her mum everything she knew about Albi and the Pisaca. *Then she'd realise what a daughter she had.*

'Hope they find Thomas,' said Rachel. 'Poor Mary Bennett...'

'He's probably run away from home to get attention. Most cases like this they're back with their tails between their legs within the week,' said Godwin, before noticing Lizzie's face. 'Are you all right?'

'Yes, *fine.*' She didn't like Thomas Bennett at all, but liked Godwin's patronising attitude even less.

'Would you like some lunch?' said Rachel.

'That'd be great. I'll pay you with that weeding session I promised.'

Lizzie looked down at Tubs to hide her panic.

'You don't have to,' said Rachel.

'Like I said, I like gardening, and you really do need some help now! And as you know I'm going to be away for a few days from this evening, going on a shoot with Jim. Plus it'll stop me feeling guilty ever since my man Chen did a runner on you.'

Lizzie knew he was referring to the Chinese student, Chen Yang, whom Godwin had *found* to help them out with the garden. The one who'd been holding on to The Book of Life in Eva's cellar. She *so* smelt a rat in Godwin. She was convinced he was up to no good. *But what could she do to stop him going in her garden?*

*

A little later, Lizzie was on her bed listening to music on her phone and fretting about everything Xing had told her the day before. At least she'd managed to call Ashlyn and fill her in about what the monk had said about The Book of Life. In return, Ashlyn had told her that she'd been doing some more research on Lizzie's family, after Lizzie's weird out-of-body experience in Louisiana.

Lizzie hoped Ashlyn would come up with a plan about the Artefacts and the so-called Unknown Realms, it was all too much for her to think about now. She was still having nightmares and scary flashbacks of her time in Cypress House with the plat eyes and Mr Paterson in the spring and she didn't think she could handle any more shenanigans with the tirthas right now.

She turned her head to the window at the sound of a spade strike into stony ground outside. Looking down at the criss-crossing hedges of the garden of rooms behind the cottage, she quickly spotted Godwin's head of silver hair bobbing up and down near the fountain. After eating lunch with them, the businessman had gone straight out to fulfil his promise – or rather *threat* – of doing a 'spot' of gardening. Her mum had taken the car off to her new hobby – a choir in a nearby village – whilst Lizzie had gone upstairs to her room to keep an eye on Godwin.

It was a surprise to hear about Thomas. Ever since he had started acting strange to her last term, following her around and asking her on bike rides and stuff, she'd suspected Thomas might be developing a crush on her. She didn't like him at all – he was way too spiteful and immature – but it was still a shock to hear he'd gone missing. Would he run away from home? She didn't think he was the type. *Too much of a scaredy-cat, deep down.* He might talk the talk but ultimately he was a mummy's boy.

So where had he gone?

She glanced out of the window. 'And where has *he* gone...' she muttered, seeing no sign of Godwin.

Mr Tubs sat up and began to whine softly. She looked down at him and saw him cocking his head. He looked somehow... *nervous.*

'What's wrong?' she said.

He whined louder. Lizzie turned and looked out of the window again, just in time to see Godwin disappearing down one of the corridors towards the far side of the garden.

'Let's go, boy!'

She tugged out her ear buds, leapt off the bed and ran through the house to her great-uncle's study. Within moments she was out of the Sun Garden's side entrance, across the brook and through the orchard with its gnarled trees all bent low with rosy apples. She came through a cast iron archway with a sun and moon at the top and stopped, listening carefully and trying to catch her breath. Mr Tubs paused behind her.

'Where's he gone?' she whispered, and Tubs began to walk forward, sniffing the ground.

'Good boy – seek him out,' she said, thinking of how it was normally Godwin Lennox doing the hunting.

She followed the little golden-haired dog as he trotted down a short corridor, clearly on the trail. They came past an entrance towards the Lavender Garden with its sunhouse, and then past a group of steel butterflies on metal poles interspersed among black-leaved bushes. Mr Tubs began to speed up and she smiled, pleased she was going to find out where the businessman had slipped off to – when suddenly she heard an alien, tinny sound. She stopped and listened.

'*...the Queen of the Damned will rule a thousand years, a thousand years will last my pain...*'

Music! Or rather, as soon as she thought about it – a mobile ringtone. Her mouth twitched as she imagined Godwin headbanging to heavy metal.

'*...all the boys that failed her...*'

She glanced down the corridor to see that Tubs had disappeared, no doubt lost in the primordial wolfish pleasure of tracking scent.

'Tubs!' she hissed, but there was no response.

What should she do? Follow Tubs and find out what Godwin was doing – or go and check out why there was a mobile phone ringing thrash metal in her garden?

'*...the clatter of fallen blades echoes across the...*'

The tone went dead. There was no response, as Lizzie guessed the voice mail kicked in.

She felt a sudden chill as she imagined *another* intruder in the garden. The first one – Lady Blane, the Pisaca – had been terrifying enough.

After a moment's reflection she thought it was more important to check the phone out than Godwin, who after all might just be heading off to fill a watering can with the tap at the Tower or something. With a final glance back at the corridor down which Tubs had disappeared – *why did he have to run off when she could do with his help?* – she doubled back and headed towards the area where the ringtone had come from.

She pushed her way down a particularly overgrown hedged corridor, spitting twigs of yew out of her mouth – *she and her mum were never going to be able to manage with this garden!* – and found herself at the entrance to a small nondescript room with a scrappy lawn. *A room whose name she couldn't remember.*

After stopping and listening for a moment – the only sounds the faint drone of a tractor in the distance and her heart thudding in her ears – she peeped around the corner.

The room was empty.

Just the long grass, dark hedges, and a thick border of waxy green-grey shrubs. *She knew there was nothing interesting in this garden, that's why she'd never bothered exploring it before.*

And then she spotted the mask in the shrubby border.

She'd never noticed that before. Her curiosity piqued, she headed across the messy lawn to the mask, which looked like one of the African ones she'd seen in the cottage hall.

As she reached it she noticed how the plants around it had all been trampled – *that must be why she'd not seen it –* and then she spotted the phone, lying beside the mask in the long grass.

She bent down and picked it up. It was a Nokia, and she pushed the button on the side to light it up. It came on in camera mode, showing her her new blue trainers in the grass. There was a small circle at the top of the screen with the last picture, so she tapped on it and saw a photo of the mask, then a darker photo of the mask, and then... *a picture of Thomas Bennett!*

His face was in profile, he was standing in the woods clearly attempting to look cool and disdainful, and from the tilt of the shot Lizzie was sure that this was a selfie. *After all, he didn't have any mates.*

A few more photos – a BMX bike decorated with flame stickers, a picture of two large black beetles grappling in the dust, another selfie but with a farmhouse in the background – and she was sure it was Thomas' phone. She returned it to the home screen and checked the calls. *Mum (48), Dad (37) Unknown (27), Brian (3)* ...

God, it *was* his phone. Lizzie looked at the mask for a moment, then up at the blue sky, and then felt herself overcome by a sudden sense of dizziness.

OH...MY...GOD...OH...MY...GOD...OH...MY...

The words kept repeating themselves in her head as she tried to absorb what she knew – *knew* – had

24

happened. His disappearance a couple of days ago. The way he was always bothering her, ever since she'd told him she didn't want to go on a bike ride with him. *The way he'd said he might come and see her anyway.*

And she'd not spent this much time in the gardens and poring over her great-uncle's painfully detailed journals without knowing a tirtha when she saw one.

That must be it, the secret of his disappearance. Thomas had forced his way in from the woods – she could see the broken branches under the hedge – and in doing so, he'd found a new tirtha. And – surely without knowing it – had activated it. It was the most obvious explanation.

Thomas Bennett had gone through a tirtha.

Lizzie felt her legs go wobbly, so she sat down on the grass. She tugged her ponytail and rubbed her nose. *What was she going to do?*

With the exception of the Kashi portal where she went occasionally to see Pandu and Raj, and the Master of Nets where she'd paid a couple of visits to Xing, she had been keeping away from the tirthas ever since her escapade in Louisiana. She felt like she'd had enough drama to last her a lifetime. No, it wasn't just that she *felt* it – she *had* had enough drama to last a lifetime. No one could be expected to do more than she'd already done. *And she wasn't even fourteen yet.*

And now Thomas Bennett had gone and done this.

What a clown! She wasn't responsible for him. He'd just have to work it out himself, whatever *it* was, the strange place and situation he'd found himself in. *Was she his mother?*

After a few more minutes thinking like this she got out her own phone and called Ashlyn. There was no reply and the voicemail was full. *Damn!*

She leaned down to have a closer look at the mossy sculpture on its wooden pole.

The mask had a large, bulbous forehead, tiny, slanted eyes and a long, narrow nose. It looked very strange, alien and indifferent, the thinness of the eyes and the deep score marks on the cheeks were scary. Very scary, she thought, remembering her conversation with Xing. *But she knew what she had to do.*

Lizzie pushed her face into the back of the mask and vanished once again from her English garden.

Chapter 3: The Boat on the Bayou

It was hot – very hot, *bayou* hot – and the boy and girl lay on their backs gazing at the white-blue sky as their boat drifted alongside the bank of the Louisianan lagoon.

'So what are you going to do with your life?' said the girl, Caroline Day, whose spray of blonde curls bushed around her head in the bow of the rowing boat.

'Me? With my life now?' said the boy, Hector Fields, sprawled at the other end of the boat, slender arms crossed behind his shaggy afro.

'No, that sleepyhead turtle over there was who I was talking to.'

'Oh, well *he's* gonna be just fine eating all the pondweed he can find for the rest of his days. Long as he keeps one step ahead of Mistress Allie and her winning grin.'

A sudden memory of *him* – Mr Paterson, the Hoodoo priest who had trapped her in time to *feed* off her blood – smiling his broad smile flashed through Caroline's mind and she shuddered, despite the stifling heat. *Thoughts returned of the fight with the plat eyes, of Lizzie and Pandu so dramatically saving her when Paterson was going to kill her right over there in that clearing, by this very lagoon...*

'Everything's so different now,' she said, saying the first words that came into her head, just to block out the awful images. 'The cars, lifestyles, culture, prospects...'

'Different but the same,' said Hector.

'Different for...people *of colour.*'

Hector laughed. 'Different. But the same.'

'But we've even had a *president...*'

'Yes, but still riots across the country. Still too many black people in the prisons. Shootings in churches.'

It was too hot to talk deep so they both stayed quiet for a while, the only sound the occasional flip of the water's surface by a fish, bird, or something else. Then Caroline said: 'Miles hasn't taken things so well.'

'Ain't no surprise. It was so... *ugly* on the inside. Being possessed by *them.* The plat eyes.'

'But you've found a way to deal with it.'

'You might think I have.'

Caroline lifted her head to look at him, squinted her eyes against the fierce sun. 'Hector – if you ever want to talk about it at all...'

'I'll let you know.'

Again they fell silent. Caroline thought about all that the poor boy and her older brother had been through at the hands of that devil Paterson. How he had enslaved them with his Hoodoo magic, possessing them with the swamp spirits and bending them to his despicable will for over fifty years of suspended time. *It was inconceivable.*

And now, after the visit of her distant cousin Lizzie, the spell had been broken and she and her brother Miles, Hector and the other men who had been made into plat eyes had all found themselves living in a different century. A different country. *How were they ever going to adapt?*

'I miss Lola so much...' said Caroline, thinking of her unfaltering carer who had died saving her. She sat up and looked across the silvery water. Everything was so tranquil, so deeply still. Like the sun had quashed the breath of every living thing.

'The way she used to... *Hector!*'

The boy sat bolt upright in the boat. 'What is it?'

'Over there – in the trees!'

He followed Caroline's pointing finger into the dark shrubs and oaks overhanging the water's edge.

'Don't see nothin'...'

'There!'

And this time he saw it – or rather *him,* the man standing in amongst the shrubs some fifty yards away. *Wearing a black hooded cloak.*

'Who the heck is that?' said Hector.

'I don't know... but look, he's following us!'

Sure enough the figure began to move quickly through the tangled mess of vegetation along the lakeside towards them.

Dark memories of the nightmares she'd experienced whilst trapped in Cypress House flooded through Caroline's mind. *It was all still so close to the surface.*

'What shall we do?' she said.

'Row out,' said Hector, grabbing hold of the oars and deftly slotting them in the outriggers.

'Caroline – it's me!'

Both children looked back at the same time, just as the cloaked figure emerged into an open area between the trees, hood falling back to reveal a tall woman with long, reddish hair.

'It's Ashlyn!' said Caroline, relief sweeping through her.

'Who?'

'A friend of Lizzie's... she's been helping me out. She comes through the tirtha.'

'Oh.'

'Row over to her.'

So Hector steered the boat back to shore, where they were met by the tall woman.

'Sorry if I gave you a scare,' said Ashlyn, as the two children climbed out of the boat.

Caroline saw that her lovely hair was wet and bedraggled around her shoulders, with flecks of green weed in it. The woman's face was smudged with mud.

'I put this,' said Ashlyn, tugging her cloak, 'in a plastic bag so I could put it on over my wet clothes when I came through the tirtha. I only realised when I came through that it wasn't the best attire for this heat.'

Caroline knew that the portal from Lizzie's English garden exited right into a deep, muddy pond a few hundred yards away across the bayou, hence the value of some fresh clothes.

'Do you want to come up to the house for some coffee – or tea?' said Caroline.

'Yes, that would be great,' said Ashlyn. After Hector had drawn the boat up on to the bank and been introduced, they began to make their way up through the sun-dappled woods, towards Cypress House.

'It's too hot,' said Ashlyn.

'There's heavy rain forecast,' said Caroline.

'Storms,' said Hector.

'That'll cool things down a bit,' said Caroline.

'How are things going?' said Ashlyn.

'Not easy,' said Caroline. 'Miles is taking it bad, he's been drinking a lot recently. We've sorted the home schooling issue out for now though. Mr Ewell – he was a plat eye too – is going to start teaching me and Hector next month. He's a well-read man. *Most* educated.'

'Good. It was going to be hard to try and register you in a proper school,' said Ashlyn.

'Yep, just wait 'til we try getting Social Security numbers for a job,' said Hector. He put on an incredulous voice: 'You is *how* old?'

'We'll have to stay in the backwoods forever,' said Caroline.

'We'll work it out,' said Ashlyn. 'One step at a time.'

It wasn't long before the old plantation house where Caroline lived came into view through the trees. A young man – Miles, Caroline's older brother, the head of the household – was sitting in a wicker chair beside a small table on the verandah, glass in hand.

'Well ain't that the height of fashion?' Miles called out as they approached, tipping his glass at them.

'Do you like it?' said Ashlyn, semi-twirling to flap the cloak up.

'I sure do. Fancy a drink?'

'Nothing stronger than a coffee for me thanks.'

Miles sniffed and looked down at his drink, his face suddenly miserable. 'Yeah,' he said.

Caroline looked up at Ashlyn and saw that the Englishwoman was gazing at her, a look of concern on her face. Caroline shrugged.

'I need to get home, my dad's expecting my help with some chores, and we're painting the outhouse,' said Hector. 'Bye Mr Day, Miss Williams – Caroline,' he added, and scooted off.

'I'll go put the coffee on,' said Caroline.

'I'll help you,' said Ashlyn.

Miles swished away a fly and then gazed back at the forest as his sister and the Englishwoman went inside.

'He needs some help,' said Ashlyn in a hushed tone as they came into the kitchen.

'Tell me about it.'

'It's going to be much worse for him than the others, because of... because of what he did to Mr Paterson. Is there a doctor you can call on?'

'No. The one we knew – Dr Braker – died seventeen years ago.'

'Let me think about it,' said Ashlyn. She stopped and took hold of the girl's arms. 'Look, Caroline, there's something I need to tell you.'

'What?'

'Lizzie's friend, Xiao Xing, has been translating The Book of Life. He's found out a whole load of stuff about what Paterson and the others were up to. It looks like they're after some objects that have been imbued with special powers. Artefacts. They need them to perform a ritual that will help them stay around on Earth for a long time. Possibly *forever.*'

'Great,' said Caroline, shaking her arms. The bright sunshine streaming in through the kitchen windows made her hair and skin creamy, almost white.

'What have you done with Sally Ally?'

'She's in my room – like always.'

'You used to keep her with you all the time.'

'I used to be crippled.'

'I've been doing a bit of research and I think she's some kind of Native American artefact, a *kachina* dancer. I think it might be one of the artefacts they're after. Remember how Paterson handled it?'

'But he's dead now. And so is Lamya, and that other one – Eva, the Picasa.'

'*Pisaca*, and yes, they are, but we still need to be on our guard. One of their helpers got away, and Pandu said that there's an Indian businessman who was in cahoots with them and is still on the loose.'

'So what do you want me to do?'

Ashlyn looked at her. Caroline's hair and skin might be as pale as could be, but her eyes were dark. Dark and *sharp.* 'Hide her,' said Ashlyn. 'Somewhere really safe.

'And watch out. Watch out all the time.'

Chapter 4: The Ghost Boy

Men with the heads of swordfish and bush buffalo and pigs and shaking and pounding hearts and cries and whoops whilst all around spin the Bantu, *the dead who are separated only by a thin skin of sky, and then...*

...her eyes were open, she was seeing, and it was just the same.

A great, shaggy creature with a black, cut, zigzagged wooden face and thrusting snout was bearing down on her, arms and legs flailing wildly, a machete slicing through the air in front of her face. Most chilling was the clear sight she had of his eyes, flickering darkness that seared into her soul. And there was thumping, a surge of people from behind, chanting, a crazy rhythm and someone, a woman, was screaming. *Screaming.*

So Lizzie screamed too, filled with terror, her hands coming up to protect her face from the machete and from those burning eyes. She collapsed back in the dust, her head striking something hard.

Everything went black.

*

There are dots all over and then shapes, black and white and grey, chevrons and zigzags and honeycombs (like the grid of the garden from above), flashing marks on the sky and then she is whirling, skidding down a dark tunnel that rotates with silver-charged shapes and as she exits the world explodes into the full wideness of mind, and she is back with the Bantu, *the people who came before, who are now, and who will come after, all those who inhabit the busy, bristling other side of now, pushing towards her with other creatures, wild cats, monkeys, huge frogs, snakes, bats, hippos, the myriad spirits of the jungle, all somehow joined within the grid of spirit world, the jewel-strung grid, and there amidst the shaking beings and beasts and the creatures that start to lose their form to more abstract shapes is a presence of warmth, familiar but unknown, a glimpse in between horns, sighs, cries and gulps, of a man, an old pale man with a white beard,* him, *and she knows,* knows, *that he is looking out for her...*

...and for a moment her eyes are open, open wide, and she is floating, floating in the air, and she can see the whole scenario below her, the conical palm-leaf roofs of the huts, the dusty clearing with the shaggy dancer in the elaborate mask who shakes himself and waves his machete above her prone body half hidden beneath a small shelter with an opening out of which a thin trail of smoke escapes, a large rectangular building behind the shelter, and all around the clearing dozens of men and women in the strangest mixture of clothes all standing around looking on in amazement, and there, in the middle of them, a woman running towards the crazy dancer and shouting *stop* and then...

Darkness again.

*

'She is coming round.'

Some light, some dark, some heat, brown walls, a window with vivid green leaves outside, *heat*...

'Here...'

She felt a hard ridge press against her lip. She opened her mouth and warm water wetted the back of her tongue. She gulped and opened her eyes.

There were two faces in front of her, a woman and a girl, both brown, both calm, both... *kind*. The woman wore a necklace of sea-green shells.

Lizzie sat up.

'Where am I?'

'You are in the village of Dehani,' said the woman. 'In Cameroon. You are safe. I'm Abena, this is my daughter, Malika.'

'But... that creature... with the dark face and... *sword!*'

'Don't worry about him, that was my brother,' said the girl. 'He was in a mask. He was dancing. What is your name?'

'Lizzie,' said Lizzie with a sigh, lying back on to woven blankets that were all that softened the earth floor.

'My head hurts,' she said. She lifted her arm across her forehead, which helped to distract her from the throbbing pain.

'It's OK,' said the woman. 'You banged it on a wooden pole beside the Sacred Fire after you appeared.'

'Er yes, about that, you see, there's this *magic* trick I learnt...' Lizzie muttered, peeking out at the woman and girl who were kneeling in front of her.

'You can stop there. We're friends of Eric.'

Lizzie sat up again, the pain in her head instantly forgotten.

'You knew my great-uncle?'

The woman smiled. 'Yes, he's lovely man.' Then, noticing the look in Lizzie's eyes, she added: 'Is he…'

'He died last year,' said Lizzie. 'It was a heart attack.'

'Oh…' said the woman, looking down. 'How sad. But I think we had started to realise, it'd been so long…'

'How come you knew him?' Lizzie could barely contain her curiosity, the surprise.

'He used to visit us,' said Abena. 'Like you, he appeared before the sacred fire, at all times of day and night. The Bantu brought him here, to help us. He saved many of our children's lives one time when a bad sickness came with the rains. He helped us with our English, and was very kind, especially with Zuri.'

'Zuri?'

'My son, Malika's brother. The boy in the mask.'

Something was pricking Lizzie's memory, something from her great-uncle's diaries. *She was sure she'd read an entry about this place, these people.* When she'd first found the diary in Ashlyn's house. But before she could think about it, she suddenly remembered what she was here for.

'Have you seen a boy? I mean, a white boy. An English boy? Appeared in front of the fire like Eric and me?'

Abena and Malika looked at each other, and just at that moment a tall boy appeared in the open doorway.

37

'Yes, we have seen him,' he said. 'You are talking of the Ghost Boy.'

Lizzie stared at the boy. He was older than her, maybe fifteen or sixteen she guessed, with a narrow head and slender, muscular body. He was wearing a bright yellow T-shirt and grey shorts. Immediately Lizzie thought how beautiful he was, but then as he glanced down at her she noticed something frightening about him, a violence in his eyes.

'Zuri!' said Abena.

'What mother?'

'Don't look at her like that, you'll scare her!'

'Huh.' The teenager shrugged and moved across the spartan hut to pour himself some water into a bowl on a small foot stool. Lizzie noticed how swiftly he gulped the water, at the same time scratching furiously at his side.

'What do you mean, the *ghost boy?*' said Lizzie, pulling herself together.

'He appeared two days ago,' said Abena.

'He stole the Nkisi,' said Zuri, suddenly standing above Lizzie as she sat on the floor. *How quickly he'd moved!*

'The what?'

'The Nkisi. It is a sacred wooden statue that connects us with our ancestors,' said Abena. 'We keep it by the holy fire, which we never let go out.

'When the Ghost Boy appeared Salomon was there with several other elders. They moved towards him but he grabbed the Nkisi, and swung it at them. Uffe said that the boy was crazy, shouting all kinds of things – but of course Uffe doesn't speak English so he did not understand.

'They tried to calm him down but he was out of his mind, swinging the statue wildly in front of himself to keep them away. Then one of the nails in the Nkisi cut Salomon and there was blood, which made everyone mad and they chased him.

'The boy trampled through the sacred fire but luckily he didn't catch fire and the flames didn't go out. Then he was off into the forest, and gone.'

'The men were too old to catch him,' said Malika quietly.

'Oh God,' said Lizzie. 'Poor Thomas.'

'Who?' said Abena.

'I think I know who your Ghost Boy was,' said Lizzie. 'He's just a farm boy from back home. Near where I live.'

'But then how was he consorting with the Bantu?' said Abena.

'Who?'

'The Bantu, the people of the spirit world.'

'You mean... how come he appeared through the portal?'

The woman dipped her head.

Lizzie guessed that Abena must think only special people could use the tirtha. *Magic people.* 'Well, I'm afraid the portal just kind of... *works*... for anyone,' she said.

Abena and Malika stared at her, whilst Zuri continued to gulp water.

'But the important thing,' she continued, 'is that his coming here was... an accident. He didn't mean to. He found the portal by mistake, I'm sure.'

'So why did he take the Nkisi?' said Zuri, accusingly.

'I guess... I guess it was just to defend himself, like Abena says. He must have felt completely... overwhelmed. Terrified.' She could imagine *exactly* how Thomas had felt, one moment stealing into her garden on an English summer day and the next finding himself confronted by African villagers on the other side of the world.

'No matter, I will catch him soon,' said Zuri. 'And because he took the Nkisi, I will kill him.'

Chapter 5: *Les Coupeurs de Route*

'He can't kill Thomas!' said Lizzie, once the older boy had left her alone with Abena and Malika.

'The elders have said he must be punished,' said Abena.

'But he's just an innocent kid! He didn't know the significance of this *gisi* to you.'

'Nkisi,' said Malika, whilst Abena looked thoughtful.

'You've got to help me change their minds!'

Abena snorted. 'Those old men? Not a chance.'

'Then what else can I do?'

'I don't know,' said Abena. 'Let me think.'

But Lizzie's mind was racing. 'You say he appeared two days ago? How has he survived since then?'

'I don't know,' said Abena. 'But we do not think he has gone far from the village. One of the women – Mama Esti – saw him stealing bananas from the back of one of the huts.'

What a turnaround! Lizzie remembered how dismissive Thomas had been about Albi, the 'feral child' lost in Hoads Wood in Herefordshire. *And now here he was, in an almost identical situation.* She tried to imagine how he would survive a night in the jungle, with no shelter or food and the noises of the animals and insects around him. *Inconceivable!*

She feared that he might even be dead already, bitten by a snake or eaten by a crocodile or... *lion?* What kind of big cats did they have in this part of Africa? Leopards? Cheetahs? *All of them?*

How would she even begin to tell people back home what had happened? And what about Thomas' parents?

Her head throbbed with pain.

'What can we do?' she muttered. Once again she had found herself right in it. *All thanks to the tirthas, the bane of her life.*

'Rest,' said Abena. 'Rest for a while. Zuri is the best hunter in our village but every trail he's found so far has ended. Until the boy is seen again there's nothing anyone can do.'

Lizzie lay back on the floor frowning. She started to worry whether Godwin and her mum had already noticed she was missing but in the next moment she was asleep.

*

She awoke to a commotion outside.

Her head felt OK so she stood up and walked towards the door of the empty hut. As she came out into the village she saw two boys – one in a football shirt and the other wearing what looked like a purple dressing gown – scamper past her. One of them noticed her and shouted something like *coopers doot.*

She headed in the same direction that they had been running, seeing an old woman holding the hand of a naked toddler going the same way too.

In between the huts she could see a small crowd gathering at the edge of the jungle.

'Lizzie!'

Her arm was grabbed and she looked round into the face of the young girl, Malika.

'What happened?' said Lizzie.

'Soon after you fell asleep one of the villagers spotted the Ghost Boy again. Zuri and another man went after him, but they were attacked by... by...what's the word...in French, *coupeurs de route*...road bandits?'

'Oh my God!' said Lizzie. 'Are they all right?'

'Zuri is but they killed Bandru. They shot him dead!'

'Oh no...'

'Stay with me,' said Malika. 'If they are still in the area and see you they will take you too.'

'What do you mean?'

'Ransom. They make their living kidnapping local herders on the plains mostly. But they'd kill half the village for a white girl. Those men are dogs!'

The two girls reached the edge of the teeming crowd of villagers. In the midst of them Lizzie could see Zuri, pushing people away and looking more wild and angry than ever. At one stage he struck a young boy who had grabbed him, causing the boy to stumble backwards before being caught in the arms of a woman. Everyone was shouting and speaking but Lizzie couldn't understand a word.

'*Arretez-vous!*'

It was an old man who had shouted, and it had the desired effect of making everyone stand still and shut up. The man was wearing a brightly coloured white and green robe, with a similarly coloured brimless hat.

'It's Salomon, the elder,' whispered Malika.

As Salomon began to speak – or rather, *rant* would be more accurate – Lizzie realised he was using mainly French but with some others words including English thrown in. She caught the words Malika had said – *coupeurs de route* – and a phrase that sent a chill down her spine – kill *le Garçon Fantôme*. Her French was good enough to know what that meant: kill the Ghost Boy.

'Have the bandits killed Thomas?' she asked Malika.

'No, but they've captured him. He's gone.'

The two girls pulled back from the angry mass of villagers so that they could speak.

'What will they do to him?' said Lizzie.

'I don't know. Most likely try and ransom him.'

'Who to?'

'Don't know. They might think he's from here – maybe a missionary child – or take him away and try to make him tell them where his parents are. They probably have a base somewhere.'

'We have to help him!'

The group had calmed down now, to allow a heated conversation to take place between Zuri and the elders. Lizzie tried to listen but her frustration deepened as she could only understand a few odd words and phrases. It looked like there was a big disagreement going on, but

44

with Zuri's restless manner she couldn't be sure that this wasn't just the way he talked.

'What are they saying?' she asked Malika.

'Hold on.'

A little later Zuri shouted something and stormed off, back into the village. As everyone started shouting again, Malika pulled Lizzie further away and said: 'The rumour I heard was wrong. The boy wasn't spotted but Zuri discovered a tree he'd been picking fruit from, a few hundred metres from the village near the road. He came back to get Bandru. They went and lay in wait for an hour and suddenly heard shouts from the road. When they went to investigate they found the boy had already been captured by a large group of bandits. They fired their guns at Zuri and Bandru. Zuri escaped, but Bandru was hit in the chest.'

'That's terrible,' said Lizzie. 'What are they going to do?'

'Nothing.'

'What?'

'Salomon and the elders say that we should let them take him. The Ghost Boy means nothing to us. But Zuri wants to go after them.'

'So he does care about Thomas!'

'No. He wants to go after them because they've taken the Nkisi.'

*

Whilst the villagers continued their discussions, Lizzie headed back to the hut.

She needed space to think. She wasn't sure how long she'd been through the tirtha – *getting knocked unconscious hadn't helped* – but she guessed it was three or four hours. It was still daylight outside, but she must have been gone for at least two or three hours, maybe more. Her mum and Godwin would surely be missing her by now, so she should go back – but how would she ever explain to them about Thomas?

Perhaps the best thing would be to get back to Ashlyn and Madeline, and see if they could help. At least if they disappeared for a while no one would miss them like she would be missed.

But what could they do anyway? How would a couple of British women hope to find and rescue a boy who'd been kidnapped by murdering African bandits? She buried her head in her hands.

The bloody tirthas had done it again.

'Girl!'

She looked up and saw Zuri towering over her. *He'd come in so quietly!*

'What?'

'Do you want to help your Ghost Boy?'

She nodded.

'Come now, then. We're going.'

'What?'

Zuri moved over to the back of the hut. She saw him pick up a bag, no, a rucksack, and begin filling it with things.

'What are you doing?' she said.

46

'Packing. We might need to spend the night in the forest.'

'You want *me* to come?' Her mind was a storm of confusion. She didn't know whether she wanted to go or not. Whether she *should* go – or not.

'No one else in the village will come. They are all cowards. Are you?'

'No.' As soon as she'd said it she felt scared. *Yes I am!* An image of her dad, her brave handsome dad with his dark stubble and gentle grey eyes appeared in her mind. *Dad, I need you...*

'You've got about three minutes to decide.'

She should go back, Ashlyn would know what to do, perhaps she could get Pandu and Raj. Her brain was a mush of thought and indecision.

'Two minutes.'

'I can't!'

'OK.' Zuri hurled a second pack that he'd been filling back into the corner. He slung the other over his shoulder, picked up his machete and a short spear – *a spear!* – and strode out.

'Wait!' she shouted, as he disappeared from view.

'Wait!' she shouted louder, diving over to grab the pack. She ran out of the hut.

And found him standing waiting for her. Tall, powerful, not edgy or fidgeting at all now. Like an image from a movie, from another world. Just staring at her with dark, inscrutable eyes.

'Come on, then,' he said.

And they left the village together.

Chapter 6: The Stranger in the Storm

The man with the silver hair walked alone through the storm.

Rain, torrential, relentless rain pounded the trees and marshy ground all around him, drenching his shirt, jacket and trousers as he stumbled onwards. A large binocular case bounced against his chest. Every so often he removed his glasses from the bridge of his nose and wiped them with his fingers, just to help him see a little further for a few moments, before once again they became completely blurred.

The ferocity of the storm was astounding. Lightning flashed and thunder crunched and ground the air. The swamp trees swung about wildly with the wind, losing twigs, leaves, and trails of moss in all directions.

The man stumbled on, his feet squelching in slippery mud and shallow pools.

Then, in a dramatic flash of white light, a house showed up ahead, in between the trees. It had pointed gables, a long porch, golden-lighted windows. And then it was gone, although now if he strained his eyes he could still see the faint glow of its electric lights.

The man quickened his pace, cursing as a low branch swung up and whipped his cheek. Soon he came to a fence which he vaulted easily, emerging from the swamp on to a scruffy lawn. He trotted forward and took two quick steps up on to the covered verandah.

Safe. With the rain no longer pummelling his head and the wind drastically reduced he took a moment to compose himself. He stepped forward and banged on the door.

There was no reply so he tried again, then found a doorbell which he rang.

Moments later a light went on, and then there was the sound of bolts being drawn, one, two, three. The door opened.

'What do you want?'

The man inside was bearded, handsome, young, with long brown hair swept back from his high forehead. There was a croaky edge to his Southern accent, and he had an oddly dishevelled look.

'I'm very sorry to intrude,' said the man with the silver hair. 'But I got lost in the storm and my phone was ruined by the rain. Could I perhaps use yours?'

The young man stared at him.

'Where you from?' *Slurred.* His voice was slightly slurred.

'England.'

'England?' *As if he'd been drinking.*

'Yes,' said the middle-aged man. 'I've been touring the States on holiday. I was staying in Labouchelle, exploring the bayou a little. I got lost in this wretched storm.'

'You were out there alone – on foot?'

'Yes.'

'*Jeez*. You Brits...'

Suddenly there was a shout from inside, down the hall, a girl's voice: 'Who is it, Miles?'

The young man, Miles Day, called back. 'Someone got lost on the bayou. Sorry, what's your name?'

'Brown. Raymond Brown.'

'Well...' Miles looked around the Englishman's shoulder as a gust of wind blew a splattering of rain on to the porch behind him. 'I guess you ought to come inside, Mr Brown.'

'Thank you!'

The man followed Miles down the warmly lit hall with its plush red carpet and delicate portraits of families and landscapes on the walls, down to an ornate living room at the far end.

In the room Caroline Day was sitting in front of the mantelpiece, clutching a leather-bound book.

'This is my little sister, Caroline,' said the young American. 'And I'm Miles. Caroline – this is Mr Raymond Brown.'

When the girl said nothing, the Englishman said: 'Pleased to meet you.' He turned to Miles and added: 'Thank you so much for answering the door, I realise it must have been a shock to hear someone at this time of night – and in these conditions.'

Caroline looked at the bedraggled man uncertainly. His clothes whilst soaked through looked expensive. She'd overheard most of what was said in the hall. *Was he really English?*

'What were you doing out on the swamp?' she said.

'I'm an ornithologist,' said Raymond. 'I went out on the bayou from my motel early this morning and got carried away with some sightings. I saw a red crossbill, very rare on the swamp, you know. Then the bad weather came in and I wished I'd brought a compass!'

'You were out on the swamp on your own with no compass?' said Caroline.

The man blushed, but said nothing.

'Look,' said Miles. 'I'm afraid we have some bad news for you. We don't have a landline anymore and our cell phone isn't working either, because of the storm.'

'Oh…' said Raymond.

There was another awkward silence during which Caroline looked the man up and down suspiciously. He looked like some kind of *aristocrat*, not a bird watcher. Then Miles said:

'Look, you can't go back out there again tonight. Labouchelle is at least twelve miles from here, probably thirteen. I could run you back there, but navigating the track in this weather will be hell and to be honest I've had a little too much to drink. You're going to have to stay the night.'

Caroline threw her brother a look of daggers, but in his drunkenness he scarcely seemed to notice, and certainly didn't react.

The Englishman's face broke into a smile. 'I'm so grateful!' he said. 'Look, I'm very happy to pay you for being put out like this.'

'No matter,' said Miles. 'Come on. I'll take you upstairs and get you a room. Then you can have a shower and I'll find you a change of clothes.'

Caroline watched as her brother led the stranger out of the room. She felt a sudden shake and weakness in her limbs, her body's reminder of all the time she had spent bent in a wheelchair.

No way was Raymond Brown for real.

*

'Wait!'

Lizzie and Zuri had barely left the village when a cry came from behind them. They looked round and saw Malika racing towards them through the trees.

'What do you want?' said Zuri, as the girl stopped before them, panting. 'Go back to the village!'

'I am coming with you,' said Malika.

'Stay with mother.'

'I want to help.'

'No.'

'You are taking *her* with you!'

'She doesn't matter. You are my sister.'

'She matters every bit as much as me.'

'You're not coming, it is too dangerous.'

'Try and stop me.'

Lizzie saw the glare in Zuri's eyes. His chest swelled as he drew in breath and looked down his nose at the younger girl. Then, after a moment, he breathed out. 'You can't come,' he said, more quietly. 'Mother's heart will break.'

'She will be proud if we bring the Nkisi back to the village. You know how much the Nkisi means to her too.'

'Mother's heart will break,' Zuri repeated.

'We will both be responsible for that.'

'What have you brought with you?'

Malika pulled a small pack from her back. 'Food and water. My penknife and some plasters. And these.'

Lizzie looked into her open palm and saw what looked like five crudely fashioned tent pegs.

Zuri immediately reached out and took the pegs from her. 'Maybe you will be useful,' he said, pushing the pegs into a leather pouch on his belt as he turned around and continued on into the forest.

'What were they?' said Lizzie to Malika as they followed him.

'Nails,' said Malika.

*

So here she was, trudging along behind a hyperactive teenager and his kid sister through the hot Cameroonian jungle, following in the footsteps of a gang of gun-toting killers who'd kidnapped a hapless Hereford farmboy.

Not how she'd planned to end her Tuesday afternoon.

And that farmboy was none other than Thomas Bennett! *Of all the people in the world who she would risk her life for...*

Lizzie glanced back over her shoulder at the mass of solid wood, creepers and spiky leaves that swallowed up the view. No chance of turning back, she'd be lost in minutes. Nothing else to do except keep on following this crazy boy to oblivion. And if she ever got back and her mum and everyone else asked her what she'd been doing all this time she'd just tell them about the tirthas. Let them become someone else's problem. *She'd had enough of them.*

But she was sure to get killed this time, she knew it. They were following a bunch of men *with guns.* Men who had already proved their capacity to murder. What in the name of sanity was she doing?

Lizzie Jones, you've really gone and done it this time.

'What?'

It was Malika who had spoken, glancing over her shoulder to look at her.

'What?' she said.

'You said something.'

After a moment looking at the girl's curious face Lizzie realised she must have been thinking out loud.

'Sorry,' she said. 'Nothing…'

'Are you scared?'

Lizzie thought for a moment. 'Not right now. Feeling a little crazy perhaps. Are you?'

'A little,' said Malika. 'Have you ever done anything like this before?'

'Well… Not like this. Not hunting down a band of kidnappers in the jungle. But – I've done other stuff. Scary stuff.'

'Like what?'

'It's kind of hard to explain, but… I helped the Indian police catch a serial killer.'

'Wha…'

'Shh!' Zuri hissed, waving his hand behind his back, and they both went quiet.

He turned to face them. 'We're approaching the road where Bandru and I met the men. They're probably long gone, but we must be careful.'

The two girls followed him cautiously towards some bushes, where they were able to peer out at the old dirt road, heavily encroached by the jungle. They all kept very still, listening carefully.

'They've gone,' said Zuri. 'Come on.'

The three teenagers walked out and stood on the road, which quickly disappeared in both directions into the trees. Lizzie noticed large tyre tracks and big soaking pits in the road, which seemed to be made almost entirely of mud, with just a scattering of stones pitched in.

Zuri was kneeling down peering into the mud.

'They went that way, towards the river,' he said. 'At least eight or nine of them, with the boy. Come on.'

They began to make their way down the road, being careful to avoid the water-filled holes and large stacks of mud.

'Those holes are the size of bath tubs,' said Lizzie. 'Do people actually drive down this road?'

'No neat tarmac here,' said Zuri.

She decided to keep quiet after that.

Chapter 7: Prosper's House

They had only been walking for a few hours and already her feet were sore.

'Are you OK?' Again Malika fell in beside her, whilst Zuri strode on ahead.

'Yes. My feet hurt.'

'Try not to think about it,' said Malika, who Lizzie noticed was walking in flimsy pumps, nothing like as sturdy as her own trainers.

'OK,' said Lizzie, then added: 'I'm thirsty.'

'Plenty of water here in the rainforest,' said Malika, diverting quickly to the side of the path and finding a large, rubbery leaf that was brimful of rainwater. 'Check in your pack, there should be a water bottle.'

Lizzie pulled her rucksack off and sure enough found an empty plastic water bottle, which Malika filled for her by tipping up the leaf.

'Thanks,' she said, and drank gratefully as they walked on. Then, because it has been pressing on her mind, she said: 'How often did you see Eric?'

'So he was your relative?'

'Yes, my great-uncle.'

'Quite often, especially when we were younger. He was good to us – me and my mother and Zuri.'

'What about your dad?'

'He died.'

'Oh no!' Lizzie remembered the passage she'd read in her great-uncle's journal in Ashlyn's cottage, something about Malika's dad having died of a horrible illness. 'My dad... my dad died too.'

'How terrible!'

'Yes, I miss him every day.' Suddenly they were both holding hands with tears wetting their cheeks as they trudged along the muddy road. Zuri strode on ahead of them, shoulders back, either unaware of the muffled sobs, or uncaring.

'How old were you?' said Malika.

'Twelve.'

'Not so long ago then?'

'No, just over a year,' said Lizzie. 'We had a lot of problems afterwards, with money and stuff, sorting things out, so we had to go and live with my gran. My mum was angry with him, too, which made it all really hard.' *Why was she telling a complete stranger this?*

'Why was she cross?'

'Oh, it's a... it's a sore...' Lizzie took a deep breath. 'Mum said he was having an affair.'

'No!'

'Yes. With his assistant. He'd told Mum he was working but actually he was on holiday – supposedly with her. And while they were away in Scotland, in the mountains... their car went over a barrier and crashed into a river.'

'You poor girl...'

Malika put her arm around Lizzie's shoulder as a light drizzle began to fall.

'Keep up!' Zuri had stopped and was looking back at them.

'Get lost!' said Malika. 'Can't you see she's upset?'

Zuri cast a withering glance at them and sighed. Then he turned and kept on walking.

'Slow down!' shouted Malika, but he carried on at the same pace.

'We'll lose him if he carries on like that,' said Lizzie, sniffing.

'Don't think about it,' said Malika. After a while, long after Zuri had disappeared down the snaking road ahead, she said: 'Do you think it's true? Was he really seeing his assistant?'

'No, I don't believe it,' said Lizzie quickly. But then she added: 'Mum is certain it's the truth. But... whilst they recovered... Dad... they never found Jane, his assistant. Although they did supposedly find something that identified her, I don't know what it was. But it definitely wasn't her body – so she might not have been with him!'

'But surely they would have been staying somewhere? A record?'

'Yes, they were both in the same hotel.'

There was silence for a moment. 'I know. It sounds like I'm desperate. It's just, it's just – he was so *good*. To me, and everyone around us! So fun to be with. Everyone loved him. He could... never have done something like that.'

'Then you were very lucky,' said Malika. 'Lucky to have a good dad.'

'When did you lose yours?' said Lizzie.

'He died when I was very young,' said Malika. 'I never really knew him.'

'So sad.'

'Yes, I suppose so. It was difficult not having a man in the house. Things were hard for our family. People were kind, but it is difficult in our village having to live without a father.'

'More than a mother?'

'No. But men have more... what's the word?'

'Hair?'

'Have you seen Mama Bene?'

Suddenly they were both giggling like mad, arm in arm, stumbling through the increasingly wet mud. They reached a point where the road turned sharply to the left around a large black rock, and suddenly Zuri appeared from behind it, his heavy machete wobbling just in front of their chins.

'Shh!'

They both stopped, the mirth dead.

'They're up ahead. Five hundred metres or so. At the river.'

Lizzie froze, her throat constricting with fear. Instinctively, without another word, the three teenagers hurried off the road and hid down in a recess at the back of the damp black rock. Just as they were sitting down

59

Lizzie noticed Malika swipe a large brightly coloured spider out of the way with her hand.

'Did you see Thomas... the Ghost Boy...with them?' said Lizzie.

'Yes, he's handcuffed to one of them.'

'How does he look?'

'That is a stupid question. How do you look?'

'Leave her alone, Zuri,' said Malika.

'We're in trouble now,' said Zuri. 'They have two boats tied up by the bridge. I don't know how we are going to follow them then.'

'What about Prosper?' said Malika. 'He might be able to help?'

'Prosper - you're right!' said Zuri. 'He's not so far away, and he might be able to lend us his boat.'

'Who's Prosper?' said Lizzie.

'A friend of our mother's – from Nkambe village. Just upstream from here,' said Malika.

'Brilliant!' said Zuri. 'I knew it was a good idea for you to come along, sister.'

Lizzie felt the yawning chasm of what was left unsaid.

'But what will we say to him? He will just tell us to go back home,' said Malika.

'We'll think of something,' said Zuri.

*

By the time they reached the village of Nkambe two things had changed. One, it had begun to pour with rain, and two, it was getting dark.

Initially the heavy canopy provided the walkers with reasonable shelter from the worst of the rainstorm. But after an hour or so it had evidently reached saturation point and they began to get a drenching from the hefty, overfilled leaves finally yielding their load to the jungle floor below. Like taking a warm shower, Lizzie thought. *Just a shame she was fully dressed.*

Her spirits were sinking to an all-time low, and she kept repeating over and over in her mind that this time, *this time,* she was not worrying. She'd been through so much, after all. Wet weather in the jungle? *Try fighting off a zombie house invasion for size.* Think through an explanation for Mum? *Why bother when time itself might have stopped, or even be going backwards for all she knew?*

It was little more than a year since she'd been filling all her spare time wandering around empty parks and shopping malls in Croydon.

How things could change.

The crashing rain and increasing gloom completely killed off all conversation and she began to get used to the dull rhythm of placing one foot in front of the other. She kept peering about hoping to see some exotic wildlife – *nothing dangerous of course* – to cheer herself up, but aside from the odd dull-coloured bird and one small creature scurrying along a branch that looked remarkably like a squirrel – oh, and of course the spider that Malika had moved – she'd seen nothing. She might as well be walking in the rain in the woods back home. Except for the heat of course. And her exotic companions. And Thomas and the evil bandits. *But apart from all that…*

She was so absorbed in the drudgery of her own thoughts that she was halfway into the village before she even noticed the smell of smoke. Looking up she saw that the trees had receded and been replaced by huts, squat buildings with brown walls and palm-thatched roofs. As soon as she realised where she was she noticed the noise too, people inside the huts talking loudly as if to make themselves heard over the rain. And each hut had its own faint light, coming through the frames of their makeshift stick doors.

'Over there,' said Zuri, pointing with his short spear towards one of the homes. They passed a pair of damp, hopeful looking dogs, attempting to shelter under the narrow eaves of a hut. One of them whined at Zuri whilst his companion's tail beat weakly against the earth wall behind him.

'Baba and Dora,' Malika shouted at Lizzie through the rain. 'They must have been bad dogs today, to get left out in this!'

When they reached the hut, Zuri opened the door and poked his head inside. Lizzie heard him say a few words to the occupants. Then he turned and beckoned for them to follow him in.

Lizzie was half expecting a hut similar to Abena's, but she couldn't have been more wrong. The space was crammed with objects – small chests, stools, mirrors, pictures, pans, zigzag rugs, a radio, a couple of mobile phones, three wooden dolls, and countless other bits of bric-a-brac. The walls were covered in bright, simple paintings of school children and elegant birds on one side, and swordfish, angel fish and whales in an undersea setting on the other. In the centre, squatting around a fire

62

that filled the whole dome with acrid smoke, were two elderly women and a young boy.

The women stood up, giving broad, gappy grins.

'Malika, Zuri, *content de vous voir!*' said the first, who had a rasping voice and oddly bright blonde hair. Suddenly Lizzie realised that she was actually a *he*. A man wearing a wig!

The man and the woman hugged the two teenagers. Then the man looked at Lizzie and said: *'Et qui est-ce?'*

'Elle s'appelle Lizzie,' said Malika. *'Elle est anglaise.'*

'English!' said the man, with a stilting accent. 'How are you? Please to meet you.'

'And you. And OK,' said Lizzie awkwardly.

'This is Prosper,' said Malika to Lizzie. 'His wife Annick, and son Cedric.'

'Head cold!' said Prosper, prodding Lizzie's shoulder. She realised with embarrassment that she was still staring at his wig. 'Lose hair!' he added, laughing.

'Prosper has been wearing the wig ever since his hair fell out,' said Malika.

Lizzie smiled.

'Sit,' said Prosper, and she sat down beside the boy Cedric who gave her a sheepish smile but said nothing.

Zuri and Malika then began speaking to Prosper and Annick in French, far too quickly for Lizzie to even attempt to understand. They kept throwing her looks so she realised that she – *unsurprisingly* – must be the focus of at least some of what they were saying.

'Are you hungry?' She looked round at Cedric, who was offering her some food that looked like large wedges of fried potato.

She suddenly realised she was starving, ravenous, *famished* and she could eat a horse or a buffalo or whatever else they ate here in the jungle. She nodded eagerly.

As soon as she bit into one of the wedges she realised it wasn't potato at all, but something squidgier and sweeter. But whatever it was, it was just fine and she gobbled it down quickly.

'Thank you,' she said, licking the tips of her fingers.

'You are hungry,' said Cedric, giving a shy grin. 'Very hungry!'

'Sorry,' she said, realising that she had been staring at his food, which was on a giant leaf.

Annick interrupted them with something, probably in French again, that Lizzie didn't understand.

'D'accord Maman,' said Cedric. He reached over to a pot near the crackling fire and drew it near to him. Then he stood up and got down a bunch of greenish looking bananas, hanging against one of the walls. Lizzie helped him to peel and chop them into wedges. Then Cedric oiled the pot and placed them on the fire to fry. Soon the smoky room was filled with a delicious, sweet smell.

As the bananas cooked, Malika came and sat down beside Cedric and Lizzie whilst Zuri continued to speak to the old couple. She spoke a little to Cedric in French, then said to Lizzie:

'We'll stay here tonight. Zuri is still discussing the boat. I don't think Prosper is very happy with his idea, but we'll see.'

Lizzie thought it was a tall ask.

*

After they had hastily scoffed some more of the banana – Malika told Lizzie it was actually a thing called *plantain* – as well as some lentil-like beans, peanuts, and small yellow tomatoes, Annick offered them dry clothes to change into. Lizzie became acutely embarrassed, until she saw that there was a wooden screen at one side of the hut where each of them in turn went to change. The damp clothes were then placed around the fire to dry out, whilst Lizzie sat on a woven rug wearing a pair of beige denim shorts blotted with ink stains and a T-shirt with a picture of the Eiffel Tower on it.

Once they were all sat around the fire Prosper produced an unlabelled bottle full of pale brown liquid.

'Hey, now,' he said, unscrewing the top. 'You drink, Lizzie?'

Lizzie looked at the bottle uncertainly as he poured some of the contents into a small cup.

'Come on, you drink, is good!'

She looked nervously at the others. Annick was staring at her, whilst Malika seemed to be hiding a smile. Zuri was frowning and picking at mud under his nails with a small knife, not even glancing at her.

'I don't think...' she said.

'Drink!' said Prosper, thrusting the cup at her.

She took it from him and lifted it to her nose tentatively. It had a fragrance she recognised, something that cleared her sinuses, even though she couldn't think straight enough to name it.

What was it? *Supposing it was spirits?* She had drunk some beer and cider before – with friends back in Croydon to look cool, and once or twice her mum had let her have a small glass of wine – but she wasn't keen on the taste and she couldn't stomach the thought of drinking something really strong.

'No, I...'

'*Continues!*' said Annick in French, in her throaty voice. She gave Lizzie a piano-key grin.

Lizzie realised she had no choice. *Talk about social pressure,* she thought – and took a slug.

As soon as she drank the slightly fizzy liquid she realised what the smell was – ginger! And it didn't taste alcoholic at all.

'It's ginger beer!' she said.

Prosper and Annick cackled away as Malika and Cedric smiled.

'People like ginger beer a lot,' said Malika, taking a cup that Prosper was offering her. 'We make our own.'

After Prosper had poured some out for all the teenagers and Annick, he produced a second green bottle that he began to drink from. After a few slugs he offered it to Zuri, who took it and drank in silence. Lizzie guessed *that* was the proper beer.

Annick then began talking for a long while in French, and Lizzie soon lost track of what she was saying.

Occasionally Zuri would make a comment, but Malika and Cedric kept mostly quiet. She was surprised given the circumstances at just how relaxed and comfortable she felt with these people. Prosper finished the first bottle of beer – Zuri hardly drank any – and was soon halfway down his second. The smoke from the fire began to sting Lizzie's eyes and she began to feel drowsy – *very* drowsy. Then suddenly Prosper stood up and took off his wig, exposing his completely bald and knobbly head. Legs astride in the midst of the smoke he began to sing a surprisingly melodic and wistful song in French.

Lizzie's brain was far too scrambled to follow the song properly, but she caught the phrase *vive la rose* a few times as her mind blended anxious thoughts about her mum and Mr Tubs with reassuring images of white flowers blossoming in fast motion. She began to sink slowly sideways on to Malika's comfortable shoulder.

Vive la rose, je ne sais pourquoi, vive la rose et le lils...

Chapter 8: The Intruder Returns

When Caroline Day awoke she was pleased to hear... nothing.

It had been a night full of noise, of whippings, crashes, booms, of creakings, bangings and crackings. It had taken her ages to get to sleep with the rain pounding her windows and the roof above her head, making her wish for the first time that she had kept her downstairs bedroom. She kept looking at the faint luminous hands of the clock beside her bed, frustrated by the time it was taking her to fall asleep. It was some time past two when she finally dropped off, but it was only into one of those deeply unsatisfying sleeps in which her mind raced with surreal images and she remained semi-aware of a distorted reality around her. At one stage she thought someone had entered her room and was coming towards her and she tried to scream as they sat down on her chest but she couldn't even find her breath and then she began to panic that she was suffocating and would die – only to become fully conscious again and realise that she had been in a kind of sleep paralysis.

Something that Dr Braker, God rest his soul, had told her about when he visited six months ago. At least, six months as she remembered it, which was actually *fifty-five* years ago.

She would never get her head round it.

But still it was bliss to lie here now in bed, with a faint light coming through the shutters and a sense of peace having descended outside.

What a storm! And what a weird evening, with the arrival of that strange man.

Raymond Brown.

After Miles had given their uninvited guest a change of clothes they had offered him the remains of a *jambalaya* for his dinner. Then they had all sat in the living room together whilst Miles and their visitor got steadily drunk – or *drunker*, in the case of Miles – on their whisky cocktails, the two men talking with increasing camaraderie about the *special relationship* between the US and UK, and the threats to world stability posed by radicalisation, rampant capitalism, and the rise of Russia and China. The only thing that kept it from being terminally dull for Caroline was her amazement and secret pride at how well her brother had got on top of all the issues of an infinitely changed world in such a short space of time. A few months ago, as he perceived it, he'd been living in 1961 when everything – with the possible exception of the deteriorating situation in Vietnam – was going pretty well under the Presidency of JFK. Now they knew the horrific end to that presidency, together with all the horrors and complexities that the modern world had chucked up since. But Miles held his own with someone who had actually lived each day through it.

And she'd thought her brother was all about his next drink.

Finally, after an hour or so, even her admiration for Miles' intelligence had reached its limits and she'd stood up and told them that she was going to bed to do some reading. And that's when Raymond Brown had said something strange, that had made her worry. *Worry more.*

'Are you all right there?' he'd asked, standing up and offering her some support. 'Have you hurt your leg?'

She had felt her cheeks flush with embarrassment and hurt pride. *Did he know something?* She had thought she was completely healed from the damage Mr Paterson had done to her body. Declining Mr Brown's offer to help her to her room, she'd hurried out.

Had he really wanted to take her to her room? *Creepy.*

As soon as she'd got upstairs she'd thought about what Ashlyn had said earlier, about taking care of her doll, Sally Ally. She'd immediately removed her from the bed, and hidden her at the back of one of the drawers beneath the wardrobe. It was one hell of a coincidence that the two of them had turned up on the same day.

The fact Mr Brown was with them under their roof combined with the atrocious storm had given her one of her worst night's sleep in ages, so she was relieved when she came downstairs and saw the pair of them in the hall preparing to leave. Mr Brown was back in his crumpled clothes, which with the exception of his jacket had been through the dryer.

'I'm just taking Ray back to his motel,' said Miles. His face was ashen, and his hair had wedged up to one side overnight.

'Thanks for all your hospitality,' said the Englishman. 'I don't know what I'd have done without you. So nice to meet you Caroline, you and your brother have a wonderful place here.'

Caroline forced a smile as the two disappeared out of the front door. After a moment she heard the sound of the old Ford motor clearing its throat then coughing into life. At least the battery hadn't gone flat with all the rain, she thought, as she headed into the kitchen. She sliced a bagel and popped it in the toaster.

A few moments later she was buried in *Jane Eyre*, chewing away on the doughy bread, when she heard the sound of a car coming down the drive.

Realising it was far too soon for Miles to be back she went up to the kitchen door and looked out of the window. Shortly, the Ford rolled into the puddle-strewn courtyard, swung round the great oak tree in the centre, and parked up in front of one of the outhouses.

She felt a shiver of revulsion when she saw Mr Brown climb out of the car and walk back with Miles towards the house. To help deal with it she opened the door and called out:

'You forgotten something?' *She may as well be hopeful.*

'No,' said Miles. 'Ray here didn't realise we're only a whisker away from Lake Marie, it was the next place on his itinerary. So I've said he can stay here another day with us while he explores it.'

'It's a fantastic spot for birds,' said Mr Brown. 'I might even see that red crossbill again. If I'm lucky.'

He smiled at Caroline but, try as she might, she couldn't smile back.

*

The tall woman in the dark hooded cloak moved quietly – almost *silently* – up the gravel drive in the moonlight.

At the end of the drive, where it swelled out in front of the squat timbered cottage, the woman stopped still for a few moments, possibly staring in disbelief at the cars parked there. The old Volvo, well that was no surprise – but the police car? What was *that* doing there?

The woman had been intending to head down the near side of the house but instead dropped down on to her hands and knees, then crawled along the front of the cottage until she was beneath one of the windows, still open due to the balmy heat of the summer evening.

The woman pulled back her hood and listened, her back arched like a cat, her long dark hair hanging down around her pale cheeks.

Inside, a woman was talking: '...two, maybe half past. I went off to my choir. Godwin – my friend, Godwin Lennox, was doing some gardening. I left Lizzie in the study, she was reading. She's always reading.'

A man replied. 'What time did you get back?'

'Around four. Mr Tubs – that's our dog – was here but I haven't seen her since.'

'What about your friend – Godwin, wasn't it?'

'Yes. He texted me around three-ish, saying he was going home. He was off on a trip with one of his friends, your Assistant Chief Constable, Jim Weston.'

'Have you spoken to him since?'

'No... no. His phone had got one of those messages, you know, the one that says they're unavailable and you can't leave a message now.'

'OK. Can you let me have the number anyway?'

'Yes of course.'

'I'll get in touch with him through ACC Weston.'

'Great. Please tell him to call me.'

'Will do. Can you tell us a bit more about the... *relationship*... between you and Godwin?'

'Well, he's um... Well, he's a friend and...'

'Partner?'

'No, well... no, not properly.'

'There's some romantic involvement?' This was another voice, a woman's. 'Sorry, I wouldn't ask unless it was necessary. Everything helps us form a bigger picture.'

'Sort of... early stages. But yes, I suppose, yes.'

'How long?' continued the policewoman.

'Have I known him?'

'Yes – and how long into... the start of the relationship?'

'Since we moved here, last November. But – romantically – only a few weeks.'

'Do you know much about him?'

'Yes, he has his own business, in agriculture, but... He's a gentleman, very kind. He's fine, honestly, very trustworthy.'

'OK,' said the policeman. 'Have you contacted everyone else she might have seen – or called?'

'Well, I've called my mother. And all her friends that I know.'

'And nothing of note?' said the policewoman.

'No. No one has heard from her.'

'OK. Keep thinking, and let us know if there are any other leads you think of.'

'Yes, yes... of course.'

'We're going to put announcements out on the local networks. Plus we'll be alerting cars on all the major roads in the area, the buses, trains. We're already organising a search tomorrow for Thomas Bennett, so we'll obviously be looking for Lizzie too. Do you know if there was any connection between the two of them?'

'You mean like… a relationship?'

'Anything.'

'Well – they're obviously at the same school together. Lizzie knows Thomas. At one stage I thought she might be…seeing him. But I think I was wrong.'

'OK, that's helpful,' said the policeman.

'Thank you for your time, I know how awful this must be for you,' said the policewoman. 'Can I just ask you one more thing?'

'Sure.'

'Do you think she might have run away from home for any reason? Under her own volition?'

Another pause. 'I... I don't know. I... suppose it's possible.'

'Were there any problems? Family problems, or such?'

'We… we had some issues. Her father – as I mentioned earlier, he died last year, in a car accident – well, that caused some difficulties between me and Lizzie…'

'Why?'

'He was supposed to be working when he was killed. But actually he was on booked holiday with his assistant. His *female* assistant.'

'Oh.'

'They were both killed. They were driving through the Highlands. The car went over a cliff and… was badly burnt up. Ended up in a river. They found more of him… than they did of her. The only way they could be sure she'd been in the car was checking the DNA of some of her teeth that had been broken out.'

The policeman grimaced. 'I'm sorry to hear that,' he said.

'Yes, it was awful. But – it sounds even worse now – I've found it hard to forgive him. It was an affair. He hadn't paid as much off of the mortgage as he'd said. He didn't have the life insurance he said he had. None of his things were in order.'

'I'm sorry. And Lizzie – she finds it hard to accept the facts?'

'Yes. She's a real… *Daddy's* girl.'

'So you argue? Is the atmosphere… difficult… at home?'

Silence. Then: 'A bit. But not terrible. Not terrible at all. But I think she finds… me and Godwin… a bit hard. And she wouldn't run away… I'm sure she wouldn't…'

And then the sound of sobs, and the policewoman saying, 'Don't worry, don't worry Rachel. You've told us all we need to know for now. We'll find her. We understand...'

'Would you like us to find someone to stay with...' began the man, but he was suddenly interrupted by a fury of barking and growling.

'Tubs!' shouted Rachel.

From inside the room there was the sound of scratching, claws slipping on a wooden floor, but the woman beneath the window didn't wait to hear any more, instead she backed up quickly, then leapt to her feet and sprinted to the side of the house, just as a small golden terrier-like dog flew out of the downstairs window and began to chase her.

The woman sped down between the kitchen and the dark branches of Hoad's Wood that overhung the fence, then into the Sun Garden, all the while with Mr Tubs snapping at her heels.

Abandoning her original plan, the woman ran down the hedged corridor leading from the Sun Garden, past the succession of small doorways into other rooms and then turned into the larger garden at the far end of the corridor. There she made a miraculous leap into the air which enabled her to clear a rhododendron bush that partitioned the area, and then she was standing before a moonlit statue of a dancing man with dreadlocks, surrounded by a ring of metal flame. She began to circle the statue and was just reaching out for it when the dog caught her up and himself flew through the air, his flews drawn back to expose his small but sharp-looking canines.

The woman hissed – a sound that seemed to rip the air, so even those inside the house heard it and wondered what it was, *a cat* said Rachel, but the policeman thought a fox – and in an instant she transformed into a foul, ferocious creature with a heavy face, twisted fangs, and flaring yellow eyes. With astonishing speed, the creature caught the small dog and flung it backwards into the rhododendron.

Within seconds, Tubs had twisted and shoved his small body back out of the bush but by the time he was back at the statue the demon's heels at which he snapped were already vanishing into thin air...

*

For a few moments, the small dog stood there, whining and growling, eyes watering. Then he turned around and headed back into the house.

He was back and asleep in his bed a while later when the woman – Eva Blane now, no longer the loathsome Pisaca – reappeared beside the statue.

Quickly, Eva began to roam the garden, her eyes wide to navigate the near-dark gloom, her nostrils flaring as she sniffed at the air trying to find what she was looking for. It was the faint citrus smell she was after, simple really, the scent of a deodorant, always the best way to find someone these days. Here a whiff of the rosy scent, then lost, then here again, becoming fainter that way, stronger this.

For nearly an hour she combed the dark garden rooms by the pale moonlight, seeking *her* out.

Finally, she stood in a small, square room, featureless except for a small border and... an uncovered mask nailed to a small stake in the shrubbery – something she'd never seen before!

'Yes!' she whispered. *This was good on so many levels.*

She knelt down and looked at the mask. It was hard to see in the shadow so she changed into demon form to draw upon the full power of her night vision.

She studied the thin eyes, as symmetrical as a scissor snip in folded paper. She studied the mossy wood, the gashes in the cheeks.

African. Mid-continent, probably Cameroon, Congo, DRC. Maybe Fang tribe. *Excellent.* There would almost certainly be an Artefact through here – as well as the girl.

And it was *so* obvious how to operate this one. Evelyn – or her stupid Arch Witch mother Hattie – must have been clean out of ideas when she hid *this* portal with her magic.

Eva reverted to human form, tucked her hair up behind her ears, and pushed her face into the back of the mask.

Chapter 9: Journey down the River

'Wake up!'

No. *Impossible.*

'Lizzie – wake up!'

Her head felt like a slab of concrete.

'Wake up, Lizzie – we have to go!' came the whisper again.

She half opened her eyes. The hut was dimly lit by the embers of the fire. Above her was Zuri, fully dressed, shaking her arm; behind him stood Malika, also dressed. Lizzie could see the slumbering bodies of Cedric and his mother on the other side of the fire, but Prosper was no longer there.

'Get your clothes on, quickly,' hissed Zuri.

'What's happened?' she asked, instinctively keeping her voice as quiet as his.

'Prosper is outside, calling our mother. Now he has slept his beer off, he has decided we cannot borrow his boat. He is going to get some men to take us back to the village.'

It was hardly a surprise, Lizzie thought. She could hear Prosper now, evidently still talking on his phone outside the hut. His voice was quite loud, he clearly wasn't making any attempt to conceal the call.

'What are we going to do?' she said.

'You'll see. Get dressed quick, he might come back in any moment.'

Lizzie watched Annick snuffling and turning over beneath her patterned blanket as she tugged her clothes on. Her top and jeans were hardly dry, but at least they were no longer soaking. When she was finished Malika handed her her backpack.

Zuri was holding both girls' arms and leading them towards the door when the curtain drew back and Prosper was standing there.

'Come on!' Zuri shouted, and ran forward.

'*Arretes!*' said Prosper, but he stepped aside when he realised the strong teenager was coming through no matter what.

'*Nous pardonner!*' cried Malika as she pulled Lizzie past the old man and out into the early morning light.

'*Revenez-vous!*' croaked Prosper, and the last Lizzie saw of him he was leaning up against the side of the doorway, frantically stroking his bald head and pulling out his phone again.

*

They were only running through the trees for a short while when they came to the river. Lizzie spotted several canoes, all drawn up on to the bank.

'This is the one,' said Zuri, grabbing one of the boats and pushing it back into the water.

'But he doesn't want us to take it!' said Lizzie.

80

'How else are we going to get the Nkisi back?' said Zuri. 'And your friend?' he added, as if it was an afterthought. *Which Lizzie realised of course it was.*

'But...' she began, and then realised he was right. It was their only chance.

Within moments the three teenagers were all in the canoe, and Zuri was kneeling in the front with his back very straight, powering them out with swift strokes of the oar into the middle of the river.

'Here we go again,' muttered Lizzie, staring back at the dense foliage of the jungle and gripping the sides of the narrow boat as it wobbled through the water. Thoughts of home again flashed through her mind.

'Oh, Mum...' she muttered.

'We'll be all right,' said Malika, touching her arm.

'I'm sure we will,' she replied. Without believing it.

*

It started off cool out on the river but as the sun appeared like a lip of lava on a distant hill the heat soon began to build.

As the morning wore on it once again became hot – very hot. Propped up in the back of the boat whilst Zuri continued rowing like some world class athlete – *or robot* – Lizzie once again began to feel drowsy. She must have dozed off for a while because when she opened her eyes again she found herself staring at something she recognised, lying on a bare patch of yellowy-brown sand, beneath the hanging fronds of a palm. It was something she knew very well, long and squat, a creature she knew

81

from stories, right from childhood, and one that she had seen before in... *zoos*...

'A crocodile! It's a crocodile!' she screamed. The boat lurched suddenly as she scrambled to sit upright.

'Sit still!' shouted Zuri. 'We're all dead if we go in the water!'

Lizzie stared at the *huge* beast, which lay flat on the bank but was watching them with one cloudy yellow-green eye. It looked nearly as long as their boat, with its dusty grey scales and half open mouth showing rows of sharp, sharp teeth. He seemed to be frozen in mid-yawn.

'Oh God!' said Lizzie, panicking. They were so vulnerable in this feeble canoe, which tipped about precariously on the eddying water.

'Stay calm, Lizzie,' said Malika, leaning round from the middle of the canoe and grabbing her by the shoulders. 'We're OK, he's not coming for us. They don't attack boats.' The partial sense of relief Lizzie felt evaporated when she added: 'Usually.'

*

Clouds began to move in around midday, and the air became closer and more muggy. They stopped for a while, pulling the boat up on the bank and sharing the remnants of some cold fried plantain, peanuts – or *groundnuts*, as Malika called them – and black beans that Zuri had taken from Prosper's house. Then Zuri pushed them out again, took up the oar, and began rowing.

'Do you want me to take a turn with that?' said Lizzie after a while, somewhat half-heartedly.

'Don't be ridiculous,' said Zuri.

Malika turned and looked back at her.

'He does loads for my confidence,' said Lizzie.

'He's got a way with girls. Take that back. He's got a way with *people*.'

'It helps me – having something to do,' said Zuri.

This was the first time he'd ever explained himself. Lizzie wondered whether he was thawing a little. She noticed a rigid black and white bird, like a heron, stood on some tree roots tangled in the river. Its neck was craned towards the water as it waited for its moment to strike.

'How often did my great-uncle Eric come and see you?' she said.

'It varied,' said Malika. 'Sometimes we would see him almost every day, for weeks on end. But then we'd go three months without seeing him at all.'

'And it's because of him that you speak English so well?'

'Yes. It's taught a little in our school. But we speak it much better than anyone else because of him. French is our main language, but because our country has been colonised by both the Belgians and the British, many speak English too. And some people in the south only speak English.'

Lizzie nodded, and then said: 'Can you tell me more about him? I've inherited his home – and his garden – but I don't really know anything about him. The one person I'd hoped would tell me turned out to be...' Lizzie wondered what she could say about Eva. 'Not who I thought she was.' She'd rather Malika didn't think she was nuts. *At least not yet.*

Malika thought for a moment, then said: 'He had this way about him, of making you think he didn't like you one bit – at least at first.

'I never knew when he first came through the portal. The first time I met him, Mum brought him into our home and introduced him to me. I was young and in the middle of a silly game, down on all fours snuffling and pretending to be a warthog or something. She said he was a *wise man* who had come to visit our village.'

Then she put on a very deep voice, evidently imitating Lizzie's great-uncle. '"Is this *your* piglet?" he said – in French, of course.' Lizzie was impressed by Malika's impression – she'd even got a slight West Country accent in there. It was great to get a feel for what he might have sounded like.

'I thought he was sneering at me, and said I was sorry and tried to behave. But I soon realised it was just his style. A way of getting me – and everyone else – to pay attention to what he was saying.'

'Which I guess you would have anyway,' said Lizzie, 'with this old white guy appearing out of nowhere.'

'Yes. I'm not sure how, but soon everyone in the village knew him. And we knew about the portal, too.'

Suddenly Zuri spoke up: 'Eric knew what he was doing. First of all he did a bit of spying and found out where Yaya, our shaman, lived. He talked to him first, and told him how our village is in a very sacred place, one of the most sacred places in the whole of Africa.

People have worshipped here for thousands, perhaps *hundreds* of thousands, of years. He told Yaya to keep the portal secret from the wider world, but told him it was OK for the villagers to know, provided Yaya ordered them not to tell anyone else about it.

'Then Yaya told us. And what Yaya said, went.'

'I never knew that!' said Malika. 'That he went to Yaya first.'

'There's lots you don't know,' said Zuri, ominously. 'You were very young.'

'But – wasn't it weird? – having this old man with a beard turn up and tell you about a magic *gateway* back to his country?' said Lizzie.

'Not for us,' said Zuri sternly, without looking back as he paddled. 'All the Bantu – all the people who have ever lived, and will live – are in the spirit world, at our sides every day. We – me and Yaya – talked about it with Eric. He said most religions share our belief in an eternal world different to ours but connected to it. He didn't know how his portal worked, but he thought it had something to do with openings into that world. And he said he thought he saw glimpses of the Bantu, as he travelled through.'

'Did you... did you ever go through the portal with him?' said Lizzie. 'Back to England?'

'No,' said Zuri.

'Didn't he ask you?'

'Yaya went once. He said the Bantu did not wish for him to go through again.' He went silent.

85

'Yaya died shortly after,' said Malika quietly. 'He died in fever, ranting about the creatures he'd seen – alongside the Bantu.'

Lizzie thought about her first transportation to Kashi, about how traumatic passing through the tirthas could be. She imagined that it could have a bad effect on...on.... a *certain kind of person*.

'So... who's the village shaman now?' she said.

'I am,' said Zuri.

Suddenly there was a thumping sound followed by cries – *human* cries – up ahead.

They had just turned a bend in the river and now, looking down a long, straight section they could see an overturned boat and several heads bobbing about in the water. Those in the river were thrashing their arms around, shouting, and a couple of them were holding sticks in the air above their heads. Lizzie noticed a couple of smooth grey rocks near the upturned canoe.

'What happened? Did they hit those rocks?' she said.

'They're not rocks,' said Zuri. 'They're hippos.'

'Hippos!' said Lizzie. 'We have to help them...'

But Zuri wasn't talking any more, instead he was steering the boat swiftly towards the near side bank. Within seconds the long view down the river was hidden from their sight as they came beneath the dark branches overhanging the water.

'But they might drown,' said Lizzie. 'Row up towards them!'

'Shh!' said Zuri, looking back fiercely at her and making her sit back in her seat in surprise.

'It's them,' whispered Malika. 'The *coupeurs de route* – the bandits...'

Then Lizzie realised that the sticks she'd seen them holding out of the water must have been their guns.

'We need to save Thomas,' she said.

'This is our best chance,' said Zuri. 'We couldn't have been luckier!'

He leapt out of the boat into the shallow water and pulled it up on to the shore. 'Come on, we'll go on foot now.'

'But Thomas might be in the water... he might be drowning!' said Lizzie. 'At least in the boat we can get there quickly!'

'No!' said Zuri. 'We'll be shot to pieces before we reach them, by anyone who gets on the bank. Or else killed by the hippos! At least if we surprise them now we have a chance of getting the Nkisi and Thomas in the confusion.'

Realising he was right, Lizzie shouldered her rucksack and hurried after him and Malika through the dense scrub alongside the riverbank. As they ran they could hear a deep bellowing – obviously the hippos – and it didn't take long before the sound of the men shouting at each other in French became much louder. Soon Zuri held up his hand for them to stop, and then the three of them moved slowly forward up to a small ridge of earth. Near the top they followed Zuri's lead in lying down on their fronts and crawling until they could peek over the top of the bank.

Below them a shallow sandy area was sculpted back from the river, the effect of a smaller stream meeting with it. The area was sparsely vegetated with only a few small trees, most of which now had grown men clinging on tightly to their upper branches, shouting desperately to each other. In between the trees stalked a massive, clearly irate, hippo, flinging back its head and exposing its bubblegum-pink mouth and giant teeth.

'Keep quiet, very, *very* quiet,' whispered Zuri.

Of all the dangerous creatures Lizzie had associated with the jungle, hippos had never been one. But now, seeing this almighty creature stomping around in the sand she realised just how deadly it was. That mouth with its huge tongue would crush you with a single bite – if it hadn't trampled you to death in the first place.

Suddenly, a shrill noise came from the far side of the clearing. Looking over, Lizzie saw that there was another figure slipping down the trunk of a fairly small tree. Whoever it was had obviously lost their footing. She realised the shrill noise had been an hysterical scream of sorts.

Then her flesh seemed to shrink as she saw who it was – *Thomas!*

The teenager from Hebley was slipping down the tree and... the hippo was heading straight towards him! *What could she do?*

'Thom...' she began, scrambling up – only to find a hand clasped across her mouth and her shoulders thrust back firmly down on to the bank. She found herself pressed beneath Zuri's strong body as he glared angrily into her eyes.

'There's nothing we can do!' he whispered, before releasing her.

As she looked back down at the scene she saw that the hippo was now trundling towards Thomas's tree as the boy continued slipping down to the ground, screaming in terror. In the mayhem the bandits were also shouting out. Then she saw one drop to the ground and raise his gun to his hip and point at Thomas...

There was the loud clattering sound of bullets being fired. Breathless, Lizzie looked on, expecting to see the teenager fall. But then she saw the hippo stop, twisting back its neck and roaring again.

She realised it was turning, probably hit by some of the bullets. The man fired more shots at it, and Lizzie winced to see the creature's flank shake as it was obviously hit again. For a moment she didn't see anything as her guts heaved and she vomited into the muddy bank. She felt Malika's arm pull her round the waist. When she looked back up she saw that the injured hippo was trotting quickly back to the river edge in retreat. Within seconds it had waded out and disappeared beneath the water.

'Are you OK?' whispered Malika, the pair of them shuffling sideways on their elbows to keep away from Lizzie's sick.

'Yes,' she said, but she could feel that her whole body was shaking.

She noticed how feverishly Zuri was scanning the scene ahead. She looked back at the clearing and saw that the remaining men were dropping from the trees and heading towards Thomas. The boy had fallen on the ground and was now crouched up in a ball at the base of the tree he had been hiding in. One of the men shouted at him and she saw the ghastly look Thomas threw at them. His face was like a zombie's, drained of colour, and even at this distance she could see he was shaking with sobs.

'He's petrified,' she whispered, feeling a grinding sense of frustration that she couldn't do anything. An image of Mr Paterson with his plat eyes and Caroline tied up at the lagoon flashed in her mind. She *had* acted then, with Pandu at her side – and they had won. *But no one in Louisiana had been carrying an automatic rifle.*

'There it is!'

She glanced to her side and saw a smile on Zuri's lips. Following the direction of his gaze she noticed that one of the men was nursing a long piece of wood, like a cudgel, in his arms.

'The Nkisi,' whispered Malika, seeing her confusion.

'Is that all he cares about?' said Lizzie, feeling a sudden burst of fury.

'Shh,' said Malika. Her eyes conveyed the importance of keeping control.

Lizzie shook her head and bit her lip and stared down at the ground. The bandits might be killers, but she was starting to wonder whether Zuri wasn't some kind of monster too. *Was all he cared about that bloody stick?*

When she looked back one of the men, the one who had shot the hippo, was pulling Thomas up by his arm.

'No!' she heard the boy cry. 'Get off!'

'Tais-toi!' said the man. He was short, with long black dreadlocks and a very high forehead. As he shook the Herefordshire boy roughly about, she saw that the man had a picture of Bob Marley on his T-shirt.

Whilst a boy shouted No *in the safe, well-known accent of home, the light in the forest changed, became brighter like there was a flare in the sky, or like the sun had started to hurtle towards the earth. Near her nose, a large ant with a matt-black shell marched forward like some kind of armoured titanium killing machine beamed down from outer space. She looked up, saw the rounded five fingered leaves above her shaking as if they were in a time lapse video – but there was no wind. Beside her she saw Zuri's handsome face, his fine cheekbones and thin nose, but his rictus grin made her think of a devil emerging. She thought of someone she knew, someone she had known and trusted. Someone who had betrayed her.*

She thought of Eva, Lady Eva Blane.

The Pisaca.

Then everything went black.

Chapter 10: A Demon Hunting

'What's he doing now?'

'Still looking through those things.'

'Binoculars.'

'That's them.'

'We had binoculars in '61 you know.'

'I know!'

'Then why are you talking about them like they're some kind of miraculous twenty-first century invention?'

Peering through the thick fronds and pink flowers of a swamp lily, Caroline and Hector watched as the Englishman, Raymond Brown, waded through the shallow waters of the lagoon in rain boots. Every so often he would stop and hold his black binoculars up and stand very still, staring up into a nearby tree or off into the distance.

'He's a bird-watcher, for sure. Let's go back,' said Hector, wiping his forehead with the back of his shirt sleeve. 'We've been here ages.'

Caroline had beads of sweat all along the top of her pale, almost invisible eyebrows and above her lips.

'Just a few more minutes,' she said.

'Just a few more minutes,' mimicked the boy. 'Just a few more minutes...'

'Look!'

Hector looked back. 'So, he's trying to call home again. I thought you said his phone got ruined in the...'

'Shh – we have to get closer. He's speaking, he must have got connected!'

Still maintaining a half-crouch, Caroline set off at quite a speed down the bushy bank, following the curve of the lake edge. Hector, who was taller, did his best to keep up without becoming too obvious should the Englishman look their way.

'Slow down,' he said, but Caroline didn't.

Eventually she left him behind, and it was a short while before he finally found her again, lying on her front at the base of a cypress tree, beyond which was an open patch of bank that she couldn't cross without being seen – if Raymond Brown looked.

As soon as he dropped down beside her, Caroline gave him a look that said *be quiet.*

Faintly, the two children heard the end of the Englishman's conversation.

'...no, you're cutting out again...yes,' he said in his reedy accent, as he waded further out into the lake. 'Yes, you're back.

'No, as I was saying, don't do anything for now.

'I know. It's a damned pain, there's nothing we can do about that, I'll have to weather it when I get back.

'Yes, Jim'll hold the line. But it's going to be tricky now if the papers are involved. We'll have to think of another story. Damn it! If I'd have known she was going to disappear I'd have held off coming here. We have so much bad luck.'

'No... you're cutting out again... hold on...'

Suddenly the two children were pressing their faces flat into the mud as Raymond Brown swung around and began to wade directly towards them.

'Yes, that's better, you're back… Yes, I'm going to stay here, yes… Yes… OK. I'll let you know how it goes. Speak soon. Good... Oh, you've cut off again.'

With one ear muffled against the dirt, Caroline guessed the last sentence was spoken to himself. She held her breath and felt her heart pound as the water swished and the man walked steadily towards them. She looked into Hector's eyes and saw equal anxiety there.

The Englishman was coming closer and closer. She realised he was probably going to come out of the water at the exact space they were hiding, where the vegetation cleared.

Then Hector gave her an intense look and jumped up.

'Hey!' shouted the man. 'Who are you?'

'Me?' said Hector, walking out into the clearing. 'I'm Hector.'

'What are you doing there?'

'Nothing.'

'Were you spying on me?'

'*Me?* No, sir. I was just on my way home.'

'Where do you live?'

Of course! Caroline realised then her friend's plan. While the Englishman was distracted, she had a chance to escape. She was the only one he would recognise.

Quickly she pushed herself up on to her hands and knees and crawled backwards to where the hibiscus and lily grew thicker.

'...just a fisherman...' She heard Hector say, before she went completely out of earshot. As soon as she was back in their original spot she peered through the shrubs and saw that Mr Brown was sitting down on the bank looking at his phone, whilst Hector had disappeared altogether. She assumed he would be heading back home, to ensure the Englishman didn't look in the direction she was going.

She realised the best thing was to go back to Cypress House. She could find Hector again later.

She was so preoccupied as she returned through the tall pines that she forgot she was following the path that led through the area that she and the others – all those who'd been trapped in Mr Paterson's time-hell – knew as *The Glade*.

As soon as she saw that small wooden cross poking from the ground she stopped dead in her tracks. It felt like someone had grabbed her throat. She struggled to breath and then in the next moment she cried out, a long cry more like a wild animal than a girl. In the distance, Mr Brown stopped and looked all about, thinking it must have been a bear or something.

Caroline fell on to her hands and knees and buried her face in the grass, right in front of the fresh flowers and the small brass engraved tablet that read:

Lola Mary Corbett, 1ˢᵗ January 1919 – 3ʳᵈ September 1961
Your Life and Love, Always Remembered
We miss you so much, Miles and Caroline

*

When Caroline got home, Miles was sitting reading the *New York Times* on the porch, a glass of bourbon perched on a stool beside him.

'Is the phone back up?' she asked as she hurried inside.

'No. I just tried to call Jack. Nothing.'

Great. So Mr Brown managed to get a signal out on the swamp but they still couldn't get one back here. *Perhaps she could take her phone out later and see if she could make a call where he was too.*

She went to the library and found her tablet and turned it on, marvelling as ever at the fine resolution and the brightness and beauty of the little machine and how far the world had moved on in just half a century. She still found it almost incomprehensible how much human knowledge, art, and opinion – as well as complete *tripe* – was now available to everyone, everywhere, almost instantaneously. It certainly beat the *Encyclopaedia Britannica* that her father had taken so much pride in – although as a lover of books she thought it would never fully replace in her affections those venerable fifteen leather bound volumes that occupied an entire shelf of the library.

Once the tablet had booted, she opened up her mail account. She began a new email and, after typing in the address, wrote:

Hi Ashlyn

We have a visitor to Cypress House, a Mr Raymond Brown – from England! He says he's a tourist who got lost in the storm but I'm worried about what you said yesterday, about Sally Ally. I've hidden her, and Hector and I have been spying on him. He claims to be here bird watching, but we just heard him make a phone call and it sounded real suspicious. Something about making up a story and someone disappearing. He mentioned a person called Jim.

I don't trust him at all, but Miles has taken a shine to him and even invited him to stay with us a second night. What should I do?

Our phones are down because of the storm, so I can't even send you this message right now, although I'm going to keep trying. I'll also try and call you. I would come through the portal but I think it's more important I keep an eye on our "Mr Brown".

Caroline x

Once she'd finished, she hit send.

Then she put the tablet down on the table, and went to get herself some lunch.

*

She had considered turning up as the Demon just for the fun of it but instead the face she produced for the astonished villagers out of thin air, lit up by firelight alone, was that of the beautiful dark-eyed Lady Eva Blane.

'Mami Wata!' shouted Salomon, the Elder, crouching and holding his arms up as if to shield himself from the cloaked spirit.

'Sois pas bête!' shouted one of the women. *'Elle n'est pas mouillée!'*

Standing in front of the shelter of the sacred fire, Eva drew back her shoulders and pulled her hood down. *No, she wasn't wet – and she certainly wasn't Mami Wata, though she'd been called worse.* Slowly, she turned her gaze from villager to villager, taking in each of the dozen or so figures who sat huddled around the second larger, communal fire. Villagers who had only a moment ago been drinking beer, singing songs, and telling stories, and who were now faced with this extraordinary apparition.

'I will not harm you,' she said finally, in perfect French. 'I have come to find the English girl only. Tell me where she is.'

'Who are you?' said a woman with frizzy, slightly orange hair, Abena, Zuri and Malika's mum.

'My name is Eva. The child Lizzie Jones is my friend.'

'How do we know we can trust you?' said Abena.

'Don't anger her!' said Salomon, snatching at Abena's arm.

'No, it's all right,' said Eva. 'It's natural to be suspicious in times like these. Sensible.'

She looked at Abena. 'Lizzie misses her father very much. He was killed in a car crash last year. Her mum is still angry with her. But I have become her friend and confidante, like I was with her great-uncle, Eric. He might have mentioned me when he used to come and visit you?'

'That's right, he did,' said one man. 'He said you were a very rich lady!'

'Yes I remember!' said another.

Abena continued to look at Eva suspiciously, whilst the Lady dipped her eyes.

'They have run away,' said Salomon after a few moments of silence.

'They?'

'Yes, your girl and Zuri and Malika – the children of Abena here. They are chasing some bandits who have taken the Ghost Boy ransom. The Ghost Boy who stole our Nkisi stick.'

'This sounds interesting,' said Eva. 'Tell me more...'

Chapter 11: Night Raid

Instead of leaving the clearing, the bandits moved a little further up the brook and set up camp with the drenched tents they had recovered. Zuri had noticed that one of them appeared to have been injured in the water, perhaps a few broken ribs or something, and they were planning to let him rest before heading on. Clearly they weren't afraid of the hippos anymore.

'It's our perfect chance,' Zuri told the two girls.

'What do you mean?' said Malika.

'You'll see.'

A little later, as Zuri was off looking for food and the girls were a few hundred metres away, setting up camp – or rather a stretched and tied plastic sheet covering three nylon hammocks – Lizzie said to Malika:

'He's going to try and get them back tonight, isn't he?'

'I expect so,' said Malika.

'I wish he wasn't always so cryptic.'

'Part of the show,' said Malika.

That made Lizzie think for a while, about how the shaman had to act to make others believe in his so called powers. *Or were they real?*

She looked back at Malika, who was on her knees in the twilight, brushing away dirt and leaves to make a space for a small fire, an absent minded look on her face.

'Are you thinking what I'm thinking?' she said.

'I guess so,' said Malika.

'We're going to go with him.'

'Uh-huh.'

'Whether he wants us to or not.'

*

By the time Zuri returned the 'camp' was prepared and Malika had started a small fire with the matches they had brought with them. They cooked something small, brown and furry that Zuri had caught and then skinned in front of them, which Lizzie prayed wasn't a rat but was so hungry she daren't ask. *Bushmeat* was all he called it. She was still feeling shaky from her blackout, the vivid memory of Eva still throbbing in her head like some kind of grisly wound.

Why had she thought about her? True, she still had plenty of nightmares about the woman – or rather, *demoness* – but this one had felt like she was actually inside her, in her mind, for a moment. *It was terrifying.*

As the three teenagers sat eating their bushmeat / rat in silence by the fire, Lizzie's mind drifted back to the conversations she'd had with Ashlyn since her weird experience in Louisiana when she'd fallen off the roof of Cypress House and knocked herself out. Whilst Lizzie had known nothing – or at least known nothing *consciously* – until she'd come round a few hours later when Pandu discovered her in a bush, she'd been dumbfounded by his story about seeing her *as a ghost* walking through the Rowan Cottage garden. She'd fervently denied it at first, but later half-memories of travelling through the bayou surrounded by a faint light, and of seeing the tirtha as a mighty shimmering vortex had flashed in her mind. And then there was something about the garden itself, *her* garden, the garden of rooms, and of Xiao Xing as a boy, *L'il Xing*, and... of Evelyn, her great-uncle's aunt.

Afterwards, when she'd talked to Ashlyn about it, the Wiccan had told her that a few special people had the ability to walk through the Astral Plane – the plane that, from her own reading of Eric's diaries and from Xing's translation of The Book of Life, Ashlyn was increasingly sure connected all the tirthas. Caroline Day was able to walk astrally too, as shown by Lizzie's first encounter with her ghostly spirit on the swamp when she was being chased by the plat eyes. Ashlyn and Madeline, two of the small Hebley coven, had also experienced astral walking themselves.

But here was the thing. Ashlyn reckoned that Lizzie herself – ordinary little old Lizzie Jones, from the *London Borough of Croydon* – was really a Wiccan, or, call it what it was, a *witch*. It was in her family, as Eric had been a Wiccan too.

Although, Ashlyn had told her, from her experience, 'active' powers could easily skip generations, as she thought they might have with Eric. Ashlyn had promised to investigate more of Lizzie's family tree, to see if she could shed any more light on things.

So it was possible that Lizzie might have some mysterious abilities – but her great-uncle hadn't. *And what about her mum?*

Freakout.

But no more *freakout* than everything else that had happened in her life over the past year.

Put it out of your mind, Jones. She wondered how much more magic, mystery, secrets and sheer terror she could keep dumping into the back of her head before... *before what?*

Before she cracked.

A drawn-out throaty growl, like someone starting an old sports car, came out of the night, immediately followed by an intolerable screeching of birds and other louder creatures.

'What was that?' said Lizzie, her guts turning to jelly – *more* jelly.

'Leopard,' said Zuri.

'Leopard!'

'Might just be a lion,' said Malika.

'Not round here,' said Zuri.

'Oh God,' Lizzie whispered to herself.

What was she doing here?

*

With all the noise of the jungle at night, the frogs, crickets, birds, and worse, Lizzie didn't stand a chance of sleeping.

During the day the forest was mostly quite still and quiet, that's how she had almost been able to convince herself she wasn't far from home, walking through an overgrown wood – a *very* overgrown wood. But my, was it different at night. All around were hoots, screeches, screams, rattles, buzzes, thumps, and clicks. It was as if everything had been waiting out the hot day just to go on the rampage at night. *Which, she supposed, they had.*

It was scary, really scary. She would be on the cusp of dozing off when suddenly there would be a growl seemingly right beside her ear. She would be startled wide awake, pushing herself up in the hammock – only to discover that there was nothing to be seen in the dim firelight. For several minutes she would strain her eyes into the dark whorls and shadows of the leaves and creepers, expecting to see a black panther come bounding out towards her. But nothing ever came, just as Zuri had mockingly told her it wouldn't before they'd all clambered up into their nylon hammocks for the night.

Despite her exhaustion, the one thing she was glad of with the noise was that she was still awake when she heard Zuri drop down from his hammock and pick up his spear, then walk off into the forest.

Immediately she scrambled out too – for a moment cursing quietly as she snagged herself in the awkwardly clinging netting – then hurried to Malika's hammock only to find that the girl was snoring gently and evidently completely out of this world.

Without any time to think, Lizzie ran after Zuri to make sure she didn't lose him.

No such luck.

As soon as she had left the faint light of the campfire, and was in the *ever so* faint light of the stars, she realised that amidst the cacophony of the jungle she didn't have a clue where he was. But she *did* know that the bandit camp was only a few hundred metres ahead, almost in a straight line. So, bedevilled by doubt and scarcely suppressed panic, she decided to carry on.

The further she got from their own camp, the louder the forest became.

A sudden hiss would send her spinning around, glancing backwards, looking upwards into blackness, convinced a python was about to drop on her. A nearby thud would have her sprinting in the opposite direction, sure that some great four-footed beast was about to jump her. The screech of a bird simply scared the wits out of her, leaving her crouching in terror.

She was wondering if she should go back – *but how would she know the way?* – when she saw a yellowish glow amidst the branches up ahead, and realised she must have reached the bandits' camp.

Out of the forest and into the fire.

She came up behind a large tree and peered around the trunk into the clearing ahead.

At once she spotted the lithe figure of Zuri, creeping forwards with spear in hand.

There were three small tents a short way from the stream, with a large fire in the middle. Two men were sleeping under blankets next to the fire. Another was sitting cross-legged beside them, with what looked like an AK-47 in his lap. From his slumped shoulders, he had clearly fallen asleep whilst being on guard.

Giving Zuri his chance.

Lizzie felt a rush of confusing emotions as she watched the older boy move towards the first of the tents. She was worried sick he would be heard and shot, *dead in an instant,* and she was furious and cursing him for being so reckless. But she was also filled with secret awe at his single-mindedness, his heroic and outrageous bravery. She felt tears prick her eyes.

She held her breath as, glancing at the sleeping guard, he stopped at the tent and carefully peeled back the entrance flap to look inside. Within seconds, he had lowered it again and was heading towards the second.

What should she do? Should she go down and help him? She realised that if she did she was far more likely to jeopardise his safety, to make a sudden noise and give the game away. She decided to stay put and watch.

And before she knew it he was running away from the tent, up and away from the camp, coming straight towards her, something long and thin in his hand.

'Hey!'

The shout had come from inside the tent, but it was those lying outside who were responding. The sleeping man with the gun had lost his balance with the shock, and was pushing himself up off the ground. But one of the others sleeping outside, the one closest to Zuri's path, was up on his feet with lightning speed, and Lizzie saw a flash in his hand as he swung a long knife at the boy.

106

Zuri's arm, the one with the spear, moved a little and Lizzie noticed that the spear was no longer in his hand. She looked at the man and saw that he was standing holding the spear himself now, like in a movie, because she realised... it was caught there in his stomach. *Zuri had thrown the spear into the man's stomach.*

And all of it happened in a second, Zuri hardly seemed to have altered his pace, the only difference was that now he held only the second object, the wooden stick, the *Nkisi stick*, Lizzie realised, in his other hand.

The second man was up from his blanket and starting to run when there was more shouting and he stopped. Lizzie looked behind him and saw that the one shouting was the guard with the AK-47, now standing up with the gun ready at his hip, and then she realised with a sudden wave of nausea that he was commanding the other man to stand out of the way so that he could fire his gun, and she looked back at Zuri running and realised that he was still a short way from the trees, a clear and unprotected target...

'NO!' she shouted, springing out from behind the tree.

It was enough. Instead of firing at Zuri the man spun round to look at her.

And began firing.

She didn't know how it happened but next she was crouching down behind the tree looking into the dark forest and all she could hear was mighty thwacks, bullets cracking into the trunk behind her head. She could feel the whole giant trunk shake with each impact.

107

She was being shot at by someone with a machine gun.

'This way – just run this way!'

It was Zuri, not beside her but a few metres off to her left, moving in the dark shrubs now.

She didn't think but jumped up and ran with him.

Bullets fired, leaves hissed, branches cracked and splintered. She bounced off her feet, snagged shoulders and clothes and scratched her head hard on something. She wondered if she'd been hit, but was still moving. She could find out if she was injured when she stopped.

They had to get away, and now Zuri was gripping her arm and men were crashing through the trees behind them.

They had to get away.

They ran into darkness.

Chapter 12: Flight through the Jungle

She had spent many years in the jungles of Borneo during the fifteenth century, when she was hunting down ancient *Bahau* ironwood figures – so moving through this one was second nature.

Eva ran quickly through the night, in human form, her cloak flowing behind her like a fold in reality. Her senses were fabulous, knitting together so that her infrared vision and heightened sense of smell and hearing were able to sift detail at a feverish rate. Amidst the near-infinite diversity of the forest, in near-total darkness, she would hone in on the finest dent in soil made by the side of a young girl's trainer, or a small snag of wool left on a branch where another girl's top had snagged. She could catch amidst a thousand earthy jungle scents the snake-thin trace of Zuri's sweat, the lemon-lime iota of Lizzie's days-old deodorant, weaker by far than in the cottage garden but still present, still making itself felt, like a genetic anomaly.

Sure – it won't let you down.

Eva smirked. Despite a few months' banishment to the Astral Plane, she hadn't lost her sense of humour.

As she ran she felt confident, so confident that soon she would have them. The villagers had spilled so much, with scarcely any need for *charming*. All of them – with the possible exception of the children's mother Abena who was far more sceptical – seemed to think that because Eva knew Eric she must be on their side. The elder, Salomon, had told her the full story – of the appearance of the Ghost Boy (Thomas Bennett, she guessed, she knew he had disappeared from Hebley), of his stealing the Nkisi, and then of Lizzie's appearance, the bandits, and Lizzie's flight with Zuri and Malika to try and save the stick and Thomas. All she needed to do was thank them and inform them she was going to help bring the children back safely. When she'd run off into the forest she could hear their cries of astonishment, how once again a few invoked the names of their primitive deities.

She could tell them a thing or two about those old gods.

The Nkisi stick was a great boon, she thought, something she had never dreamed of finding so soon, one of the bona fide Artefacts of Power that she and her followers could use at the Fountainhead. Heaven knows, they needed a bit of luck now getting the last few Artefacts together, as the draw of the Unknown Realms grew stronger day by day. Yes, it was the Nkisi that excited her most now. As for all the children, well all they amounted to was a... *snack*. A very tasty snack, after all that tortuous time away from this juicy world, her whole being broken up in the more chaotic and fragmented Astral streams.

Except for Lizzie of course. She was a witchkin, and as such a clear backup to their first choice, Charles Day's

110

daughter. Being of a younger generation than Caroline, further down the lineage from the Arch Witch Hattie, the power wouldn't be as strong in her veins – but she would almost certainly do. *Ninety percent.* And besides, Eva couldn't let her back in the village, it was obviously impossible now for both of them to be in Hebley. She would have to take her somewhere else. Probably back to her seat in Hundora, where she could put her in one of the dungeons and where she could keep Papadris happy. *The old Slav Lich would enjoy plaguing her.*

She had been following the trail for a few hours now, first along the appalling mud track that the villagers had called a road and then as dawn came to the outskirts of the second village. There she'd spotted the strange man with a bleached woman's wig out in the early light milking a goat. Thankfully she hadn't needed to address him as she'd found the trail again, only a short way away where the children had left, presumably after staying the night in the village.

Eva followed this on a slight downward gradient for a short way – but then stopped as her phenomenal demon powers began to fill her with a sense of...*foreboding.* She listened carefully and then she heard it, as faint as blood sloshing in the ear. Her skin flushed as she ran on for a few hundred metres to find her worst fear confirmed.

A river.

At the peach-coloured bank she saw the marks where the boat's keel had been, the prints of trainers and flat-soled hemp shoes in the mud.

Frustration and anger ripped through her face, contorting it briefly into the malformed shape of the demon. She cursed, cursed aloud Uncle Casimir, the Teutonic Knights, *Hattie Swift*, everyone she had ever fought and hated.

A river, and a boat. The two things no hunter, whatever their skill, could cope with.

The children had escaped.

She pulled at the trunk of a large *ayous* tree, two, three times until finally the whole thing snapped and it fell down with a mighty splash into the river.

That made her feel slightly better. She sat down on the bank, and engaged five hundred years of cunning and hard-won wisdom to try and solve the problem. She knew how she was going to get inside Lizzie's mind, that was obvious, the girl had exposed her weakness to her within a week of their meeting. But whilst it was good to break their spirits, that wouldn't help her to actually *find* them.

A short while later a loud whooping started in the treetops and Eva Blane had her plan.

*

After running through the dark damp jungle for what felt like forever, the teenagers finally stopped.

Lizzie grabbed her thighs and sucked in breath, staring at tiny stars that flashed in the blackness where her feet and the ground should be. She felt sick again, but this time she didn't heave.

Suddenly there was a rasping sound and she looked up to see a match flaring into life. Zuri touched it to something fine, like spider's web but mossy, and it burst into bright yellow flame. He dropped it on to the ground, so for a few moments they were all able to see properly, to look into each other's eyes and see the state they were in.

Zuri had a gash on his arm, with dark blood forking down from it like a lightning strike. Close against his side, he held the long, gnarled wooden club, struck through with dozens of giant, black-looking nails.

Malika, whom they'd collected on their way, was exhausted, slumped against a tree, eyes closed, her shoulders heaving up and down as she tried to regain her breath.

Alongside the terrible stitch in her chest and stomach Lizzie could feel a soreness on the top of her head. When she touched it she felt the congealed texture of blood. She must have cut her head on something while she was running.

She began to cry.

'You... all right?' said Malika, panting. Zuri was rummaging around, doing something in the bluish, pre-dawn light.

'Yes,' said Lizzie, although she couldn't control her sobbing.

'At least... we're... alive,' said Malika.

'They *shot* at us,' said Lizzie. 'They nearly killed us.'

'Something to tell...your...grandchildren.'

Lizzie fell down on the damp ground, continuing to sob.

'We didn't get...Thomas,' she said.

'Here,' said Zuri. 'I've put up the first hammock. You get in, Lizzie, get some sleep. I'll have the next one up in a moment for you, Malika.'

Because she couldn't see properly, Zuri took Lizzie's arm and led her to where he'd managed to hang the hammock. As he helped her into it she was grateful that, despite the terror as they fled, Zuri had been focused enough to grab all their meagre equipment from the camp before they'd kicked out the fire and carried on running. It had been a risk – a huge risk – but one she now realised was worth it. They would die in the jungle with no shelter and nothing to sleep in, she was sure of it.

As soon as she was in the hammock her head swam and she realised with each wave that she was going to pass out.

Just as she was losing herself she heard Zuri speak softly into her ear.

'Thank you. Thank you for saving me.'

And then she was gone.

*

'Thanks Mr Wislop.'

'No problem,' said the tall bald man, passing Caroline a large parcel full of potatoes and vegetables. 'Jimmy caught a nice 10-pounder bass this morning so I've put a cut in there in some ice for you too. Be sure to have it this evening.'

'Thanks again,' said Caroline, as the black man gave her a smile before turning and walking back to his truck. As she watched him go, she experienced a sudden giddiness, remembering Jake Wislop when he *wasn't* Jake Wislop, when he was someone possessed by a plat eye spirit put there inside him by Mr Paterson. She let it go quickly, because it was too weird, too creepy to hold in her mind.

But as she turned to go back inside she thought again about her brother. How was he ever going to cope with his past? It was hard for the others, for Jake and Jimmy and Hector – Hector, God he was just a boy when he'd been possessed – but none of them had actually murdered someone. *That legacy was Miles' alone.*

And she could see it in his eyes, his mouth, his hunched shoulders, every day of their life together. *She could smell it on his breath.*

She took the food parcel into the kitchen. As she unpacked its contents into the fridge and cupboards she wondered if they would be able to continue forever like this, as a little self-contained community supporting themselves with just their own skills and labour. There certainly seemed to be enough food for everyone – fish and gator caught from the swamp, blackberries and swamp cabbage from the forests, potatoes, chicken and eggs from garden plots – but it was the increasing need for electricity and modern comforts that was the challenge. So far they had been able to get enough hard cash by trading some of their surplus food with the villages and towns around, as well as by selling things like the beautiful hand-crafted oak beds and chairs that Jimmy made with his son Hector. But from the sums which Caroline did for them they knew they couldn't go on like this forever. Not considering the constant rising price of electricity and gas. It was only a matter of time before someone was going to have to work out how to get back on the grid and land themselves a proper salaried job.

And what about her? She didn't want to spend the rest of her life here in Cypress House. She wanted to travel the world, to see different people and places. And that was going to require money, and a passport, and a proper identity.

Once again she wondered if the tirthas would be their – or at least *her* – salvation.

In the other room she heard someone moving. Thinking it must be Miles, she walked through the double doors into the lounge.

Raymond Brown was kneeling down in the corner, looking into one of their glass-fronted cabinets.

'What are you doing?' she said.

He looked up, startled.

'Sorry, I was just... looking for a drink,' he said as he stood up. 'The door was open, I hope you don't mind...'

Caroline noticed that he wasn't wearing any boots, just beige diamond-patterned socks. Fleetingly, she thought how much they looked like rattlesnakes.

'What sort of drink?' she said.

'Er – a scotch or something?' He smiled.

'You're back early,' she said, wondering where Miles was.

'Yes, I wasn't having much luck. One or two things of interest – but otherwise all a bit quiet.' Then, after another awkward pause, he added: 'The door was open, I hope you don't mind that I...'

She looked down at his socks.

'I took my boots off,' he said, smiling. 'They were terribly muddy.'

They stood in front of each other for a few moments before Mr Brown broke the silence: 'Where's your brother?'

'I don't know,' said Caroline hesitantly. 'I haven't seen him for a while.'

'Oh.'

She looked at his eyes, grey and shiny, slightly magnified in his gilt-edged glasses. He was looking at her, a little too intensely. For a moment she remembered how Mr Paterson had looked at her, with such assurance in his deep brown eyes. *Such power.*

'I'll go see if I can find him,' she said, and hurried out of the living room.

'Thank you,' she heard him mumble.

But she wasn't having that mock-humility English thing. *She wasn't having it at all.*

And she wanted to find Miles. *Now.*

She ran down the corridors and, hearing a slight movement, dived in through the library doors straight into her brother who was coming out.

'Whoa, hold on little sis,' he said catching her by the arms and holding her back. 'What are you running for?'

'He's searching our house!' she exclaimed.

'Who?'

'Raymond Brown! I just found him in the living room searching through our things!'

'What do you mean?'

'He was down on his knees, peering into the drinks cabinet...'

'He was probably just getting himself a drink...'

'No. She's right.'

They both turned to see the Englishman standing behind them in the corridor.

Holding a small pistol in his hand, directed at Caroline.

Chapter 13: On Alone

'Lizzie.'

She opened her eyes to daylight, to a still canopy of greys, browns and greens. Tears welled in her eyes as she held her breath and listened, listened intently to her heartbeat, listened for that voice.

But it didn't come again.

In confusion, weeping silently, she realised she must have dreamt it.

Dreamt of her dad, softly speaking her name.

Lifting her head up from where she lay suspended in her hammock she spotted the still sleeping forms of Zuri and Malika in their own hammocks nearby. Since they weren't moving she allowed herself to give in again to tears, deep lung-gripping, diaphragm-squeezing sobs that she wrestled with to keep herself quiet.

Her dad was dead.

The one man she knew she could have relied on to sort out this whole damned mess, to protect her and sort out all the chaos of the tirthas. The one man who could have kept her heart safe. And he wasn't with her anymore.

The only place he still existed was in her mind, in the deepest fabric of her heart.

It was unbearable, and she was expected to bear it.

By who? she thought. Who expected her to bear it? *Why should she bear it?*

She could go and find the river and chuck herself into it.

That would sort everything.

Wouldn't it?

No.

Her final act could not be a betrayal of all her dad stood for. Passion and courage and adventure.

And... doing the right thing.

Although her mum didn't think that's what he was about. *Could her mum have been...?*

No, never. Her mum was wrong about so many things, why should she be right about *that?*

Cry, Lizzie, cry...

She was still crying when she heard Malika cough and groan, and then a few moments later swing out of her hammock and land on the ground.

'J'ai faim,' she heard the girl mutter, then go rummaging in her backpack.

'Je vais chercher quelque chose,' said Zuri, placing a hand on his sister's shoulder. Lizzie hadn't even heard him get out of his hammock.

Wiping her eyes quickly on her sleeve, she climbed down and went over to Malika. Zuri had already slipped off into the forest. He was like a chameleon, quickly lost to his surroundings.

'Here,' said Malika, sharing with her a few peanuts she had taken from her pack. 'Not much, but Zuri will get something.'

'Thanks.' The two girls sat down on the damp ground. Lizzie stared ahead into the crowded, misty forest. It was so densely *green,* she thought, but amidst the foliage she did spy a tiny plant with delicate pink and yellow flower nubs, growing across a fallen tree.

'Have you been crying?' said Malika.

'Mm,' said Lizzie.

'Hardly surprising, with all we've been through.'

'It's not over yet,' said Lizzie. She didn't want to tell Malika what had set her off.

'I know.'

'Do you think they'll still be coming after us?'

'No. Your friend is all they're interested in, he's their ticket to the big wide world.'

'What about the Nkisi?'

'They don't care about that. It's not worth a hundredth of what they could get for the Ghost Boy.'

'How do they get their ransom?'

'They'll probably be heading somewhere remote but that still has a signal,' said Malika. 'Then they'll ring the family and start making demands.'

'I wonder what he's been telling them?' said Lizzie.

'They're going to think he's cracked up,' said Malika. 'Perhaps bitten by a rabid monkey!'

'How are we going to explain things if we ever get home?' said Lizzie. Again she felt a hotness in her eyes. *What was happening to her?*

121

She felt Malika's arm round her shoulder, then the girl rested her head against her neck.

They were sitting like that when Zuri came back with a bulging bag.

'No meat today,' he said, 'but I did find these.'

He upturned the bag in front of them and several large dark green things fell out, the size of pears.

'Avocados!' said Lizzie.

'Yes, I found a tree.'

'That's good,' said Malika, as she and Zuri began slicing them open with their knives.

At home, Lizzie wouldn't touch an avocado but now she happily bit into the slimy green fruit.

'Even if we don't get any more food, they'll keep us going until we get back,' said Malika when they'd eaten their fill.

'Yes,' said Zuri, suddenly standing up. 'Come on, let's get going.'

He began to walk off into the jungle, the Nkisi stick tied across the back of his pack. Briefly, Lizzie noticed that it wasn't just a wooden cudgel – there was a squat face looking out miserably amidst all the old dark nails.

'Wait!' said Lizzie, standing up too. 'Aren't they that way?'

'Who?'

'The bandits?'

'Yes,' said Zuri, continuing to walk in the other direction.

'But we have to go back,' said Lizzie. 'They've still got Thomas!'

'I came to get this,' said Zuri, tapping the top of the Nkisi over his shoulder. 'My work is done.'

'But you can't leave him with them!' said Lizzie. She ran and caught his arm. 'They might kill him!'

Zuri shook her off, glaring down at her. *'Il ne signifie rien pour moi,'* he said, then turned and carried on.

'No!' shouted Lizzie, as Malika came up beside her. 'You can't do this!'

'Watch me,' said Zuri, without looking back.

'No!' she shouted again. 'I saved your life!'

'Zuri!' said Malika.

'Come on,' said Zuri, glancing back at his sister. 'We have to get home.'

Lizzie looked worriedly at Malika. 'I can't leave him,' she said.

'OK,' said Malika. Zuri was about to disappear again into the trees.

'I'm staying with her!' shouted Malika.

The boy stopped and looked round angrily. 'You're coming back with me!' he shouted.

'No I'm not.'

He drew in a deep breath, looking fiercely at the girls.

'I need to get the Nkisi back to the village,' he said. 'You do what you like.'

And he turned and strode off into the gloomy forest.

*

For a while the girls stood there, watching the trees and hoping that he would reappear. The silence of the early morning rainforest was broken only by a weird

123

ratcheting sound, which Lizzie suspected was some kind of bird.

'He's not coming back,' said Malika finally.

'No.'

'Come on, then,' said Malika. 'Let's show him what two girls can do.'

Lizzie nodded. She felt less confident than she'd ever felt before. What could they do against a group of trigger-happy bandits? *If they ever found them again, and didn't just get hopelessly lost in the jungle and end up as breakfast for a leopard.*

They untied their hammocks and folded them into their backpacks, then set off in the direction that they had come from the previous night. Shortly they ascended a low hill and the trees became sparser.

'I couldn't be his sister without learning a few tricks about hunting and tracking,' said Malika, looking over towards a bluish haze of mountains in the distance. 'We keep an eye on the sun and as long as it's on our left – during the morning – that'll make sure we're going in the right direction. We'll either reach the river or hit the stream they camped by. If it's the stream we'll follow it down until we reach the old campsite, then see if we can get any signs of which way they went.'

'OK.' Lizzie nodded, but she could see that Malika was nowhere near as confident as she sounded. Was she really prepared to risk everything just to help her? She felt a sudden deep admiration for this girl who she'd only known for...two days. *It felt like a year.*

'You don't have to go on with me,' she said as they started down the other side of the hill back into the endless rolling rainforest. 'It's very dangerous. You don't have to take the risk.'

'I know how dangerous it is,' said Malika. 'I know that this crazy thing is probably going to be the last thing you and I ever do. But I'm sticking with you.'

'But why? You hardly know me...'

'That's true. But I knew your great-uncle, someone who did more for me – and my family – than I could ever repay. That's why I won't be leaving you until... until we're through with all this.'

'You said Great-Uncle Eric taught you English but... that's not so much, is it?'

'He did not just teach us English. He was so much more than that to us. Our father died when we were very young, no one knew what of but people now think he had Ebola. Luckily he didn't infect anyone else because as soon as he started all the terrible coughing and... *bleeding*... he took himself off into the forest and was never seen again.'

'That must have been so hard for you,' said Lizzie.

'I guess – but I was only four at the time, so I don't really remember. I only have one proper memory of him, sitting on his knee as he made up a pipe. I remember it because he'd lost most of his fingers on one hand, and the way the remaining nubs prodded the tobacco into the pipe head made me think of an old, clambering turtle.'

Lizzie smiled.

'So I don't remember ever missing him. But of course, the real hardship came from not having a man in the house. Men are still kings in our village, the women have come on a bit with the school and the government education programmes, but not enough. It was very, very hard for my mum with us – until Eric came.'

'So he taught you lots of things?'

'Yes, language, ethics, history, culture, a little science – and he even got us a mobile phone. But it was much more than that. The villagers thought he was very important – *spiritually* – because of his appearance through the portal. Like I said, they believed he was in league with the Bantu, and because he made special friends with us that more than anything gave us our status. Plus of course he was a real help to me and mum with managing Zuri and his crazy behaviour.'

'It all makes sense now,' said Lizzie. She thought for a moment, then added: 'Can you tell me more about these *Bantu*?'

'Well, it's just the word we use for the *people*,' said Malika. 'But it means more than just the people alive now. It includes everyone who has ever lived, who lives, and who *will* live. We all exist in the spirit world together, it's just that we who are on the earth now can only see the others with the help of our shamans and their magic.

'That's what the Nkisi is all about,' she added. 'There is an old, old ancestor spirit bound up in that statue. When someone bashes a nail into it, the spirit can be called on to go out and do their bidding. That's how we protect our village from evil spirits.'

126

'Do you really believe that?' said Lizzie.

'Yes.'

'Then why didn't Zuri use it to kill the bandits and rescue Thomas?'

'I don't know,' said Malika, shrugging sadly. 'Perhaps because they don't pose a threat to the village anymore.'

'What?' said Lizzie. 'You mean he would let his own sister go off into danger rather than do what he could to stop her?'

Malika looked at her. At that moment, Lizzie hated the teenage boy more than ever.

*

By mid-morning it was raining, a light but somehow very *wet* drizzle that eventually drenched them through and forced their waning spirits even lower.

They came to a stream and followed it down hopefully through a dank, misty corridor of giant black stones – but it finally disappeared into a black hole at the foot of one of the rocks, leaving them no better off. Lizzie wasn't at all sure that they weren't now completely lost, and that Malika wasn't just refusing to admit it.

'Where to now?' she said as they stood beneath the towering rocks, looking down the arm-length hole where the water splashed away underground.

'Umm,' said Malika. She looked around the broken stones at their feet, and then up at the slabs of rock on either side of them, up into the falling rain.

And then she cried:

'Lizzie – run!'

Lizzie looked up and saw that several dark, hunched shapes had appeared at the tops of the rocks on either side of them – monkeys!

'What...?' she began, but Malika grabbed her arm and was pulling her back up the small valley, away from the large creatures. She began to run too, but when she looked back up she saw that the monkeys – *no, chimpanzees, she was sure they were chimps, but God, how much bigger they were in real life than in films!* – were bouncing heavily down and off the rocks towards them.

She wanted to ask Malika whether the chimps would hurt them but the sudden chorus of hooting and screeching all around them left her with little doubt about that. But why...what would they do to them? *Eat them?*

'This way!' shouted Malika, and they scrambled up a narrow passage where the rocks had broken and slid down. As Lizzie stumbled up behind her she saw giant chimps bouncing from hands to feet on either side of them, closing in rapidly. *They didn't have a chance.*

When they reached the top of the rocks and were back at the level of the trees, Malika snatched up a fist-sized rock and passed it quickly to Lizzie.

'Hit them, hard as you can!' she yelled, pulling out a knife from her belt and turning to face the two giant creatures that were now almost upon them.

Malika roared at the chimpanzees, who bared their ferocious yellow canines and bounded forward, straight into the two girls.

128

Lizzie felt herself flying backwards as one of the monsters collided with her. Somehow she grabbed on to it and hit it on the back of the neck with the stone, but it was a feeble blow. Next thing she knew she was down on the ground on her back and her chin was knocked heavily by the creature's toes as it ran across and over her.

She spun round and leapt to her feet as the chimpanzee skidded to a halt in the brush and turned to head back towards her. From the corner of her eye she could see that Malika had not been so lucky and her chimp was now on top of her, lifting its hefty arms high to pummel her. She also caught a glimpse of two more of the apes bearing down on them.

Then she had a sensation of something massive breaking through the trees, and there was a loud sustained blaring noise.

This was it. *They were going to die.*

The chimp thumped its giant wrists down on Malika's chest, and the girl shrieked in pain. The other ran towards Lizzie and she swung her rock at it, hitting it in the side of arm and seeing the chimp suddenly fly away sideways, off towards the trees.

'What...?' she muttered, wondering how on earth she could have hit it that hard, but at the same time she took in the huge mass of greyness in front of her and realised that something else altogether was happening, another beast, an *elephant*, was coming out from the trees right in front of them and its trunk was flailing about wildly and then the chimp on top of Malika was thumped aside and rolling away into the scrub only to quickly recover itself upright and stand roaring and snorting at the elephant which now stormed forward, head down and trumpeting again, a deafening sound, and the chimps which had been coming up behind the vanguard were scattering as the elephant tipped its long sharp tusks at them and then all the chimps were breaking up, bounding away, springing into trees, scattering across rocks, escaping into the forest, fleeing in awe and terror of the Lord of the Jungle...

Lizzie stood there, frozen, watching the elephant as it slowed to a trot and then stopped, close to the edge of the miniature ravine. She could see that it was watching down along the rocks, about in the trees, checking that all the chimpanzees were gone.

Was it coming for them next?

She ran and knelt down beside Malika, determined to help her up and get her moving – *perhaps they could hide in the undergrowth, she thought desperately* – and then she realised that the girl wasn't moving, and her eyes were closed.

'No,' she whispered, glancing back at the elephant, which was slowly turning back towards them. 'No...' she hissed again, seeing a large cut on the girl's forehead. Her eyes blurred with tears as she tried to stand, tried to pull the girl's inert and surprisingly heavy frame away with her, towards the bushes.

Hopeless. It was hopeless.

Everything was hopeless.

She gave a final tug then realised that she wouldn't be able to move her. The elephant was almost upon them. She sat down, spreading her knees out to either side of Malika's head.

Crying, she looked up at the beast, its smooth brow and dark, wrinkled trunk. The small, impenetrable eyes that took her in as it swung its great head slightly from side to side.

'Come on then. Why don't you just kill us now?' she said in a small voice, bowing her neck. She stared down, and continued talking to herself, to the closed eyelids of the girl whose face she was holding in her hands, between her knees. 'Come on, what do I care, I've met elephants before, it'll be easier if you kill me, I won't have to rescue Thomas, why should I care if he lives or dies, it'll be easier this way, no more bandits or *coupeurs de route*...'

There was a rustling in front of her, but she carried on talking.

'No more need to explain things, work things out, no more of these *bloody tirthas* and all the bloody problems they cause...'

'Lizzie.'

She looked up and slowly shook her head in disbelief. The elephant was gone.

And Zuri was standing in front of her.

*

'You stupid oaf! Move! *Ramses, move...*'

Nearly eight thousand kilometres away in the hot city of Kashi, the Indian boy dug his heels into the sides of the giant elephant on which he was perched. The elephant, which had been heading down Godowalia

Road when it had suddenly stopped and stood stock still in the midst of the busy afternoon traffic, did not respond. It just stood there with its head down encircled by a mass of cars, buses, bikes and rickshaws, all blasting their horns and ringing their bells, whilst their drivers screamed at the top of their lungs.

The boy, Pandu, leaned forward and spoke firmly into one ear of the gargantuan creature:

'Ramses, move *now* or it's no apples for the next year!'

And then, just as suddenly as it had stopped, the elephant lifted its head, swung its trunk twice from side to side, and began to walk on again.

A dozen horns ceased their blaring and two cyclists staggered their bikes sideways as the great animal went on its way.

'I'm so embarrassed! Why did you stop like that?' Pandu said. 'I'm sorry!' he shouted to the furious upturned faces all around him. 'I'm so sorry...'

The boy leaned forward and whispered into the creature's ear: 'If you're hoping for early retirement that's *not* the way to go about it!'

But there was no answer, of course, and the elephant continued to carry his rider on towards the Temple of Ganesh as if nothing at all had happened.

Chapter 14: Hilili Kachina

'What's this all about? We don't have any money you know.'

Miles moved forward and stood in front of his sister.

'I'm not after money,' said Raymond Brown, pointing the gun at him. 'It's something else I want.'

'What?' said Caroline.

'A special object. An artefact that I know you have.'

'An artefact? What are you talking about?' said Miles. 'Come on,' he added, stepping forward slightly, 'just put that away...'

'No!' Mr Brown raised the gun slightly, enough to make them both realise he was serious.

'I believe she –' Mr Brown nodded at Caroline, 'used it as a doll. "Sally Ally" she called it. Where is it?'

'You were looking for it last night, weren't you?' said Caroline. 'During the storm, I heard you...'

'I'm not here for a chat,' said Mr Brown. 'Just show me where it is.'

Miles looked down at his sister, and she noticed how bloodshot – *but not fearful* – his eyes were. 'Look, if that's all he wants, let's just give it to him,' he said. 'It's just an old rag doll.'

Caroline nodded. 'Come on then,' she said. 'She's upstairs. I'll take you to her.'

'Good.'

Caroline's head stormed as they moved through the house with Mr Brown holding the gun behind them. She thought of what Ashlyn had said to her, and wondered if there was an electronic reply waiting for her on the phone or tablet. She wondered where Hector was, whether he was on his way round after the incident by the lagoon. She wanted to know who Raymond Brown really was. She wondered what Lizzie was doing right now. *She wished she'd taken the witch's warning more seriously, and asked Ashlyn to stay with her.*

'What do you want it for?' she asked as they made their way up the grand staircase, where only a few months ago she and Lizzie had hurled a random array of household objects down on to the heads of Mr Paterson and the advancing plat eyes.

'Just get me the *Hilili*,' said Mr Brown.

'The *what?*' said Miles.

'Hilili. Hilili Kachina. It's a Native American Snake Dancer doll,' said Mr Brown.

'Oh, I get it, you're one of those fanatic collector guys,' said Miles, but Mr Brown didn't answer.

Caroline knew he wasn't. She remembered how Ashlyn had used that word too, *kachina*. This was somebody who had been in league with Mr Paterson, a prospect which filled her with dread. She knew that she mustn't let him take her doll, at any cost. She had to think quick.

'It's in my room,' she said, pointing down the landing towards the far end.

They reached her door and Mr Brown motioned at her with the pistol to open it. She turned the handle and led them in, her eyes immediately darting to the wardrobe drawer where she'd hidden the doll.

'So it's down there, is it?' said Mr Brown, seeing her eyes move.

She nodded.

'Go and get it.'

Caroline walked over to the drawer on her own. She knelt down in a rectangle of sunlight, streaming through motes of dust and warming the rich red-brown varnish of the mahogany drawer, its black heart-shaped handle. She reached forward and tugged at it.

As usual, the drawer came out at an angle and stuck halfway. She could feel the intensity of the Englishman's gaze on her back as she lifted it and pulled again. This time it came open all the way and she leaned down to reach her hand right into the back.

No one in the family ever knew why, not her father Charles nor her brothers nor any of the servants, but the drawer on the left of this wardrobe had been built only half the depth of the unit with a half-height back board, meaning that a small object could be placed on the floor behind it and never discovered. When she was younger Caroline had hidden things there that she didn't want Lola to find, things which as she fleetingly remembered them now made her smile because her nurse would never have had any interest in them anyway. A small gold bracelet that she'd looted from her dead mother's dressing table, the blackened gold woven like a rope; one of her father's old lighters that still smelt of char and petrol when you flicked open the silver top.

She felt the feathers on the top of Sally Ally's head, reached in further and grasped her body. Slowly, she manoeuvred the wooden doll out.

'Here,' she said, standing up and holding Sally Ally out towards Mr Brown.

'You hold on to it,' said the Englishman.

'What? I thought you wanted it,' said Caroline.

'I do,' said Mr Brown. 'But it's not all I want. You're coming with me too.'

'Hold on, now,' said Miles. 'That's not happening.'

The Englishman swung the gun at him, a look of ferocity on his face like a cornered animal. 'You don't have a say in any...' he began.

He's going to kill him.

Caroline heard the words in her head and realised without one iota of doubt they were true. This stranger who called himself Raymond Brown intended to kill her beloved brother, the one piece of certainty she had left in this crazy world.

As soon as she realised that she threw herself forward, in between the two men.

There was a muffled bang as the gun went off.

*

Like fireworks blazing then cackling into nothing in the night sky, Eva Blane felt her connection with each of the apes fizzle out one by one.

She lifted her head from her palms and stood up from the riverbank on which she had been perched for several hours, unheeding of the brown waters rushing past in front of her, ignoring – *at least until the last moment* – even the large crocodile that had at one stage emerged from those waters to check her out. She stood up, quickly processing all that had happened.

She was deeply concerned. On one level, the apes had let her down, failing in their mission to capture Lizzie and the Nkisi and bring them back to her. But more disconcerting was *how* they had failed, due to the sudden appearance of the elephant.

With her five hundred-year-old demon's instincts, Eva knew such things didn't happen by chance. Someone – *or something* – had intervened. She suspected that it was a power linked to the tirthas, action enabled at a distance by the Astral Plane, much like her control of the chimps – but she had no idea who had done it, or why. *And she hated that.*

But, she reassured herself, on another level the apes had been successful. They had found Lizzie. Maybe not the Nkisi statue, but the girl was a good start. Eva had already started working on the girl's spirit, preparing it to be ground down much further in revenge for the part she'd played in her banishment last year. And now she would be with her soon, as soon as she had rested herself after all that intricate, energy-consuming domination of the chimps. And then she would mete out proper justice to her. After that she could find some more creatures of the forest to go searching for the Nkisi on her behalf.

She was confident this leg of her journey would be done within a couple of days, and then she could get back to Hebley and reunite her band of – *frequently hapless, it had to be said* – followers for the next stage of their mission, the capturing of the final Artefacts.

Transforming into the demon, she knelt and ripped off the hind leg of the butchered croc. Peeling off the leathery skin, she gorged on the tough meat until the cleaned bones fell loosely to the dusty ground. Then she climbed up into one of the ayous trees, found a good strong branch, and fell asleep.

*

'Is – is she going to be all right?'

Lizzie looked down at the cut on the side of Malika's head, which was already swelling up like a mango. It had been ten minutes since the chimps had gone, but the girl had still not opened her eyes.

Zuri lifted his head up from his sister's chest. 'Her heart is beating OK. But who knows what this blow to her head has done,' he said.

'Is there anything you can do?'

'Yes.'

'What?'

He reached over his back and pulled off his pack. Loosening the straps, he drew out the Nkisi.

For the first time Lizzie got to look at the statue properly. The figure was standing and leaning slightly forward, eyes closed and cracked-tooth mouth agape. His hands were grasped together in his lap, and in the centre of his chest was a small, cracked mirror. All over his torso, upper arms, knees, and around his chin, jutted dozens of large, flat, rusty nails, bashed just far enough in so that they didn't fall out and instead gave him the prickly look of a balding hedgehog. A balding hedgehog *in great pain*. The Nkisi statue was grotesque, and just looking at it made Lizzie feel queasy.

'Get me that stone over there,' said Zuri, pointing at a large black rock by a tree.

Lizzie went over and knelt down to lift it. It was surprisingly heavy, and took her a moment to wrest it free from the soil. Underneath she recoiled at what she at first thought with its black and bronze stripes was a snake, but then realised was a large millipede. She hurried with the stone back to Zuri and found him crouching down, rubbing dark smudges of soil around his eyes.

'What are you doing?' she said.

'Preparing,' he said. 'As best I can.'

When he had finished circling his own eyes he used the mud to make several horizontal strikes across Malika's blue T-shirt. He then pulled his own T-shirt away from his sides and tied knots in it on either hip. Finally he reached into the pack and drew out one of the large nails that Malika had given him when they left the village. He put it to his mouth and licked it, then found a place for it in between the forest of other nails in the neck of the Nkisi, which was now lying flat on the ground. He held it there lightly whilst he picked up the rock in his other hand.

'What are you going to do?' Lizzie asked again, but this time he didn't reply.

Instead he began to make harsh sounds and noises in a strong accent, which she could barely be sure were words at all. He repeated the sounds several times crouching and shaking beside Malika's prone form, clasping the nail in one hand and the rock in the other.

Lizzie noticed that it was raining again, increasingly heavily, and steam was rising up around them from the hot earth. There was a strange, mesmeric intensity to what Zuri was saying, to how his jaw shook with the abrasive sounds he uttered, whilst all the time his gaze remained fixed on his unconscious sister. With the crash of the rain on leaves and soil, the softening of the emerald forest with the growing mist, and the dark, wounded figure of the Nkisi lying like a strange sentinel beside Malika, Lizzie started to feel light headed, distant from the scene.

'*Venez à moi, esprit d'ancêtre...*'

There was a movement in the trees, and Lizzie spun to see nothing but mist. *Just leaves*, she thought, images of pythons, chimps, prowling leopards in her head.

'*J'ai besoin de votre aide...*'

Suddenly Zuri lifted his face into the rain, opened his eyes wide, and struck the rock hard against the nail.

Everything became a blur. A low wail like the wind in an old house started up and the colours of the forest morphed and softened into smoky yellows, blacks and browns. Suddenly Lizzie saw the Nkisi spirit, she saw it, a rake-thin curled African man with an oval ashen face and mask-like flat eyes, even teeth like cut wood, and he was running, running quickly with a slight zigzag motion towards her, making her scream, screech aloud, and then he stopped

140

in front of her and studied her face as his head shook and fizzed and blurred, except for his black holes-for-eyes which she felt burning into her, sliding into her soul like a filet knife, deftly connecting with her pain, her joy, her hope, her loss, the totality of her, *then he shook his arm, his quivering fingers, off into the forest as if he was pointing, and there came the wind-wailing again and the Nkisi ran back past Zuri to the prostrate body of Malika which bending down he grabbed and shook, and shook again, and then he fell forward into her, and as soon as he did so like the back of the mind he was no longer apparent, gone – but not gone.*

Lizzie heard a scream, a girl's cry of agony. She looked at Malika but her mouth was closed. Instinctively she looked sideways into the steamy forest, in the direction in which the Nkisi spirit had pointed – and saw someone else standing there, tall and straight and still, in between the dark bushes.

It was a girl, a girl in white dress, a girl with translucent skin and dark eyes, and a mass of white-blonde, curly hair. *A girl Lizzie knew well.*

'Caroline,' she said.

The girl stepped forward from the trees, towards Lizzie. Her smile could not conceal the gravity, the deep concern in her eyes. Then her mouth moved but no words came out.

And yet Lizzie heard.

We are gone, Lizzie. It is you they need now. Take care, my friend, take care.

And then she was gone.

141

For a moment, Lizzie stood in shock, rain streaming down her forehead into her eyes. Then she heard a weak voice say: 'What – what happened?'

It was Malika.

*

The man stood holding the gun, staring at the carnage before him.

At his feet lay the bodies of Cypress House's occupants, of Caroline and Miles Day. Caroline lay on her back, her eyes closed and her face soft and still, a small, poppy-like bloom on the front of her dress. Miles lay a little behind her, on his front, a lot more blood showing at the back of his shirt.

He had shot and killed them both.

He had known that Miles would need to die, but he had never meant to kill the girl too. They needed her, the closest descendant of the Arch Witch Hattie Day, for the Final Sacrifice, which he had always known would be done by Eva. *He had certainly never intended to kill a child himself.*

If only she hadn't jumped forward at the last moment, in a foolish attempt to save her brother. He hadn't been able to stop himself from pulling the trigger, and had watched in horror as her dark eyes found his in hope and fear, before glazing over. She fell backwards from him on to the floor.

For a moment, Miles and he had both stood in shock, staring at the body of the girl lying in between them. Then her brother had cried out in anguish and rage and run at him, causing him to fire twice into his body. Miles had fallen forward on his front, and not moved again.

'Come on, man, pull yourself together,' he said to himself. He pulled out a handkerchief, wiped his cheek and brow. Then he tucked his gun into his belt, and walked tentatively forward. He prodded each of the bodies with his foot, just to be sure they were dead. Then he went over and picked up the Hilili Kachina from where it lay gazing blankly at the skirting board.

He looked at the doll, gruesome but inert, with the revolting snake in its mouth. *How had Caroline ever loved such a foul thing?*

Then he went out of the room, forcing himself to glance quickly back at the dead body of the girl.

What had he done?

Chapter 15: The Warrior Shaman

'So what made you come back?'

Lizzie and Zuri were sitting a short way away from Malika, who had dozed off again after eating some of their remaining avocado and bananas.

'Weakness,' said Zuri. 'I realised I couldn't leave my sister to die in the forest.'

'Is that how you see it?' said Lizzie.

'Yes.'

'So you think love is a weakness?'

He looked her in the eye, his habitual restlessness calmed, and she felt weak and overwhelmed again. He seemed to see straight through her. She looked down.

'I have no time for it,' he said.

'Yet it made you come back,' said Lizzie quietly.

After a few moments of silence, interspersed only by the piped squeaks of some distant forest creatures, Lizzie said:

'So what are you going to do now?'

'Will you come back to the village with me? Now that you've seen how dangerous the jungle can be?'

'No. I've got to do everything I can to get Thomas back. I don't like him, but I'm his only hope.'

'You don't even *like* him?'

'No, he's always been mean to me. Although I think now he has a crush on me. Whatever, he doesn't deserve this.'

Zuri thought for a moment then said: 'In which case I will come with you.'

Lizzie tried to stop a smile, but she felt the corners of her lips move – and knew that he had seen it too. She felt her face go hot, sweltering in the sweltering jungle.

'Can we use that again?' she said, pointing at the dark, stooped figurine. 'Can we use him, the Nkisi spirit, to smash through them and free Thomas?'

Zuri shook his head slowly. 'No – or at least not yet. There are many things you need to weigh up before using the power of the Nkisi. In this case there are two of importance. One, we don't know where our enemy is now. And two, we have just used his full power, very successfully, and as such he will not take kindly to being called on again. At least not right away.'

Lizzie thought and then said: 'So if we carry on, track them and find them in a day or two's time – we might be able to use him then?'

'It's possible. But there are no guarantees. This is the Spirit World we're dealing with. Anything might happen.'

Despite his words of caution, Lizzie began to feel something she hadn't felt for a very long time – a glimmer of hope.

'Don't get carried away,' said Zuri, and she flushed, aware that he had been reading her expression again. 'How often do you think people get randomly attacked by a group of chimpanzees in the forest?'

'I'm guessing not very,' she said.

'No. I've *never* heard of it happening. Something strange was at work, some power. Something darker than I've ever experienced.'

She stared at him.

'Much darker,' he said.

'But what about the elephant?' she said.

'I don't think that was luck, either,' he said.

'Then what was it?' For a moment, an image of Ramses IV flashed in her mind, trundling down a Kashi alleyway as she was surrounded by female Daginis.

'I don't know. Perhaps some other force. Perhaps someone, something on the lookout for you?'

'Me?' She wondered.

'Has anything like that ever happened before?'

How much could she tell him? She realised that, with things this desperate, she may as well tell him everything she knew, all her secrets. After all, it wasn't as if he didn't know anything about all the crazy stuff that lurked behind everyday reality.

So she told him everything, starting with the Pisaca's appearance in her garden and the discovery of the portal to Kashi, going through to getting trapped by the plat eyes and Mr Paterson in Louisiana, to Li'l Xing's translation of The Book of Life and then how she came through this portal after discovering Thomas' phone. She even told him about the surreal out-of-body experience she'd had when she fell off the roof of Cypress House, and how Ashlyn had said Lizzie might have some supernatural powers herself.

146

She spoke for what felt like ages, fully expecting him at first to tell her to shut up or to stop *creating* (one of her mother's favourite words). But he didn't, he just listened intently to all she had to say, watching her carefully with his fierce brown eyes.

Despite her occasional bursts of enthusiasm as she described key events – the beating off of the plat eyes on the stairs at Cypress House, the discovery of the second portal to Easter Island – she found that the overall telling of the story made her feel sad, at times even desolate (*how could she ever come to terms with the death of Lola?*), and she finished up not with a bang but by just kind of...*trailing off*:

'...so I came here, just trying to get Thomas back home. I've no idea what I'll do with him if – against all the odds – I'm successful, he's not the kind of kid who'll be able to deal with all this, he's bound to tell everyone, and then... Then, well, I'm just not sure how it's all going to end up...'

She glanced quickly up into his eyes, unflinching as ever, then looked down. She guessed he must think she was a complete nut now.

'Lizzie.'

She looked up at him.

'When I first met you I thought that you were a foolish girl, chasing after someone you had a crush on. Now I see I was wrong. You are a Warrior, and perhaps even a Warrior Shaman.'

She wasn't sure exactly what he meant by that, but the fact he wasn't criticising her – *for the first time* – meant she couldn't help but smile.

'You mean you don't think I'm crazy?'

'No, not at all. I am impressed, I don't know anyone who has been through as much as you. You are a strong person, Lizzie Jones.'

Her face and scalp felt like they were roasting, she could feel sweat prickling on her skin.

'Thank you,' she said, quietly. She thought about the other people who had told her how good, or brave, she was, including Ashlyn Williams and Caroline Day.

For a moment, thinking back over all she'd done, she could almost believe it was true.

*

A short while later Malika woke up again. Whilst admitting that her head still felt sore, she refused to rest any longer so they gathered their things together and set off again through the humid forest. After a couple of hours, thanks to the orientation skills of Zuri, they found the place where the bandits had camped by the river. It didn't take long for the boy to pick up the trail of where they had headed back into the jungle, largely because of the dense creepers and undergrowth around here which had meant the *coupeurs de route* had had to make heavy use of their machetes.

They followed the bandits' trail for the rest of the day through this bushy, overgrown landscape, all the time going upwards, so that soon they were in the foothills of the nearby mountains. By late afternoon it was raining hard again. Zuri was sure that they had made good time on the bandits, and that they would catch up with them on the next day if nothing changed.

They stopped about half an hour before dark and set up their plastic sheet and hammocks. The rain made it impossible to light a fire, so they ate more avocado, nuts and banana, and then each climbed into their hammock just as the darkness became complete.

'I think it's been long enough,' said Zuri, as they each settled themselves against the springy nylon mesh. 'I will try the Nkisi tomorrow morning – the bandits can only be a short way ahead, and I think he has rested long enough.'

Lizzie smiled to herself in the darkness. Perhaps everything was going to work out OK. *She deserved a lucky break, after all.*

She thought she would never sleep with the loud noise of the rain on the thin sheet above her, but as soon as she closed her eyes she was gone.

Chapter 16: Devastation

'Lizzie.'

The breath she drew in as she woke was the gasp of shock.

It was him, his voice. *Again.*

'Dad?'

In the hushed, pearly morning light she glanced at her companions, Zuri and Malika, but both remained deeply asleep in their own hammocks. She twisted out of her own netted bed, dropping to the ground. She looked at the softly lit forest around her.

No one. There was no one there.

She must have been dreaming – *again.*

But why did she keep hearing his voice so close to her? Why now?

And then, suddenly, she noticed a movement at the edge of her vision.

She spun round and was just in time to see the limb of a large spiky-leaved bush shaking – as if someone had just disappeared behind it.

Who – *or what* – could it be?

Her brain still felt fuzzy from the troubled night's sleep, and her limbs were tired from all the trekking. Perhaps that, the fact that she was only half-awake, was why she couldn't fully shake off the belief that *her dad had just spoken her name in her ear.*

She walked over to the spiky bush, looked beyond it into the deeper jungle, tangled with vines and creepers, crisscrossed with alive and rotten wood.

And stood absolutely still, watching.

'This way, Lizzie.'

Her heart launched itself up her chest as she twisted sideways, searching a section of the jungle she had not been watching.

And saw the back of someone, stepping away into denser scrub.

Someone in a white shirt, with their sleeves rolled up. Khaki trousers. Short-cropped brown hair, she was sure she had seen, just before he disappeared.

It was *him!* Despite all the impossibility, it was him! *She knew it.*

She ran towards the foliage in which he'd disappeared, her head a solid block of emotion, of primal hope and primal love. Of *need.*

It was him.

'Dad!' she said, as she burst through the screen of shrubbery.

And saw her father.

He was standing, perhaps ten metres away, waist deep in greenery, a vine hanging down in front of him and partially obscuring his face and chest. But it was *him,* she recognised his clothes, his shape, the way his jaw came forward a little, strong and always on the verge of that sweet, sweet, *precious smile* that she loved so much...

151

'*Lizzie,*' he said, and his head moved slightly away from the vine so they were looking eye to eye across a no man's land of foreign jungle.

He smiled and stepped back slightly, behind the vine, behind a tree, and was gone.

'Dad!' she shouted it now, and began to run, her young face an explosion of joy and hope and tears. 'Dad!'

She reached the vine and grabbed hold of the tree, twisted herself around its sharp bark to look beyond.

He was there again, about the same distance away!

Standing, this time almost completely visible, his arms hanging down at his sides, looking at her calmly.

'Dad...'

As soon as she began to walk towards him she became aware that he was not the only person in her line of sight. A motion made her glance right, and there she saw a second figure, coming out from behind a tree.

It was a tall, slender woman, with long brown hair that fell halfway down her back. Her skin had a tanned, slightly golden hue, and her eyes were deep set and heavy-lidded. Her arms were bare and somehow particularly bronzed and attractive. She wore a simple blue and white cotton dress.

The woman glanced at Lizzie, a strong, knowing look, and then carried on walking across the scene, in the direction of her dad. Her movement was smooth and elegant, making Lizzie think briefly of a deer or gazelle.

Her mind a torrent of confusion and bafflement, Lizzie looked back at her dad who smiled at her once again and then turned to face the woman who was coming towards him.

'Dad...?' Lizzie began to walk forward, towards the man she loved most in the whole wide world – and then saw that his attention had completely gone from her, as he now looked tenderly at the approaching woman. The *very beautiful* approaching woman.

'Jane, my love,' he said, opening his arms.

As the woman's arms came up to embrace him, Lizzie felt a blade of pain strike her in the guts, slip up through her chest and finish in her heart. Her dad kissed the woman.

The pain intensified inside her, to a searing pressure inside her head.

Her whole world was over.

She was dead.

She was dead.

*

'Lizzie!'

She could feel her face, her whole face crushed by livid, cancerous anguish. She couldn't open it up, couldn't open her eyes on the light of the world.

What might she see?

Besides, there were flames inside her, flames that were roasting and destroying her.

And she wanted to be destroyed.

'Lizzie!'

It was him, the African boy, not him, him, *him*, her father.

What had her father done?

The African boy had been important to her, very important – she sensed a quickening feeling about him – but she didn't need or want him anymore.

She wanted this.

A fresh hell.

Oblivion.

*

And then there is an almighty crack, and amidst the dark savage flames everything becomes alight.

She is alone in a shocking heatscape, blackness at its edges, white fire swirling around white crystal rocks.

No, she is not alone.

There are demons here, the lithe, twisting female demons known as Daginis, hissing at her, displaying their lurid tongues. There are warped homunculi, small goblin-shaped men whose skin is saturated, steaming with too much water despite the terrible heat. She knows they are the spirits of the bayou, the plat eyes who possessed and abused the men and boys in Louisiana. In the distance there are others, and there – there! – is the one she knows most, the horrendous form of the Pisaca, Eva Blane, the storm demon whose power is unutterable.

This is it, this is where they live, their home. It is terrible, but it is not terrible too – because someone else is coming. Something.

For an instant she thinks of a beast, a large, steady beast of calm, of infinite balance – an elephant, of course, but winking with a boy's eye, and her heart warms with the thought of the Indian boy, Pandu, her heart – but then the thought vanishes and she realises there is something else coming, leaping across the torched land like one of those wolf spiders, something with skinny limbs,

154

jumping about, running towards her, nimbly avoiding the repulsive demons that abide here.

Her head shakes as she watches him, trying to catch his erratic, non-erratic movement, to be sure of who he is.

The Runner. Spirit Man.

Bantu.

Man-In-The-Stick.

Nail Man.

And then his smokiness is upon her, the white-mask face with the wood-cut teeth and gashes-for-eyes is before her own face, standing, blurring in his infinite strangeness...

...and he takes hold of her

...stops a shaking she didn't realise she had

...and she feels a feeling, a good feeling, a feeling of love, and knows

...knows the love

...that, above all else, was her dad's gift to her

And then, slowly, with infinite gentleness, the Nkisi Man lets her go.

Chapter 17: The Hex

When she opened her eyes next a moment of calmness was quickly displaced by a flurry of random thoughts. It was as if everything inside her was a kaleidoscope of memory-feelings, and her first task was to re-order them.

'Where am I?'

Suddenly Malika was there, her hand on Lizzie's damp brow.

'You're OK, you're safe,' said the girl.

'My dad... what happened?'

'We don't know. We woke to a shout, and came and found you a short way off in the trees,' said Malika. 'You were lying on the ground, shaking – as if you had a fever.'

'A fever?'

'Yes. It was enough for Zuri to invoke the power of the Nkisi. We thought... there's no point in hiding it, you were in so much pain, your temperature was so high – we thought we might lose you.'

She held a small flask to Lizzie's lips and tipped it up. The water was wonderful, dissolving the dryness, unsticking her tongue from the roof of her mouth.

After a few more sips, Lizzie sat up.

'It was so strange,' she said. 'I saw my dad... in the forest... over there – it was great! But then... then there was this woman...'

Malika put her arm round her, wiped a tear from her cheek.

'They hugged each other, and kissed... and then I must have passed out. I was in some kind of hell but... the Nkisi man – the Nkisi man! He came to me, he actually helped me.'

'Good,' said Malika, holding her again.

'Yes,' said Lizzie. 'He helped me out... from the darkest place.'

'Yes, he did,' said Malika, and kissed the top of her head.

'But why... how come I saw my dad?'

'I don't know,' said Malika. 'Zuri thinks there is a witch at work on you.'

Lizzie thought for a while. A thought of the Pisaca popped into her head. She remembered then, seeing the demon in the midst of a burning landscape.

'One thing's for sure, though,' said Malika. 'What you saw was not your father.'

*

A short while later Zuri reappeared from the forest. He nodded acknowledgement to Lizzie that she was better, and said:

'Good news. I spotted the bandits climbing a grassy hill a few miles ahead. We should catch up with them tomorrow.'

'Can we use the Nkisi?' said Lizzie.

157

He looked at her. 'Not now,' he said. 'We had a more urgent need for him this morning.'

She nodded slowly. Last night everything had seemed on the verge of coming together. Now – *once again* – it was falling apart.

*

They set off again at a fair pace. Lizzie tried to ignore the pain she was getting from the blisters on her feet, and the itches from the whorls of mosquito bites on her ankles and calves. More, she tried to put out of her mind the flashbacks of her dad with the long-haired woman.

Trudging through the soft rain, she tried to work out what on earth had caused her to have such a vision. *For surely that's what it was, her dad was dead, there was no way he could have suddenly appeared in the jungle, could he?*

Under normal circumstances, she could have stopped herself there, she realised. But these weren't normal circumstances, were they? These were circumstances *plus* tirthas and a whole Astral Plane which in its uttermost extremes seemed even able to alter the flow of time. What if her dad was trying – somehow – to reach her?

The thought made her giddy.

Then she remembered the woman – Jane, he had called her, surely Jane *his assistant*, who he'd been on holiday with in Scotland when they killed. Remembering her, and the way she had seen them kiss, made Lizzie feel even more giddy, verging on sick. Anxiety gnawed at the pit of her tummy.

She couldn't cope with this – not on top of everything else.

She looked up from her feet to see Zuri in front of her, trudging doggedly on through the muddy forest. Right in front of her face was the Nkisi, half hanging out of the teenager's pack. His blank eyes seemed to stare at her, even when she moved position slightly. The blackened, bobbly nails in his neck and behind his ears were disgusting. She wished he'd stop looking at her.

Maybe *he* had caused the vision of her dad? Maybe it was an evil vision, to break her mind? What if the Nkisi spirit hadn't healed her at all, but instead was playing games with her, to grind her down?

And he was Zuri's *thing*, what if Zuri – and Malika, for that matter – were both working together, trying to send her mad? She felt her mind turn, like when she'd been on the cork-twister rollercoaster at Alton Towers, everything going topsy-turvy. *What was she doing in this place?* Was she really trying to rescue that creep Thomas? She didn't belong here, she couldn't trust anyone.

The hair-like tendrils of a creeper brushed against her cheek and she shuddered, looking up at the tangled mass of leaves and branches above her. For a moment they all seemed to move closer together, shutting out the light, and she had the impression that the whole forest was bearing down on her, set on twisting into her hair and face and she snorted angrily, desperately. It was as if the greenery itself was thinking, planning to… to what? *To trap her limbs and suffocate her slowly with its repulsive tendrils.* She felt an urgent need to get out, to escape – but where could she go?

She glanced sideways into the forest, wondering if she ran whether she would be all right. Surely if she just headed in a straight line she'd get to the river and eventually back to the village and the tirtha? Then she could get back. *But get back to what?* To her mum, who would be mad at her like always? To her dog, Mr Tubs – but what could he do for her, he couldn't even talk? *Fat good a lick would be now.*

Trudging in the wet and mud, a thousand miles from home, she suddenly felt the terrible grip of panic.

There was nowhere she could go. *She was trapped in this miserable jungle.*

Suddenly she slipped, for no reason, her ankle just wobbled and turned, and she was down on her knees in the mud. There was a shooting pain in her foot, and she cried out in anguish.

'Are you OK?' said Malika, crouching down beside her.

'Leave me alone!' she shouted, clutching her ankle.

'I just asked,' said Malika.

'Have you hurt it?' said Zuri, looking at her foot.

'What does it look like!'

She noticed brother and sister glance at one another.

'Why don't you two just carry on and leave me here?' she said.

Again Malika and Zuri looked at each other, before Zuri said: 'We'd be going home now if it wasn't for you.'

'Go home then – I don't care!' She could feel frustration and anger swamping her.

'Lizzie...' began Malika.

'Leave me! Just me leave me alone.'

'We can't do that,' said Zuri.

Lizzie noticed that he was frowning, and also that the rain had got heavier. Everyone was wet through, and her hair was sopping and stuck to her head. *Again.*

'This place!' she said. 'Does it *ever* stop raining?'

'There's a reason why they call it the rainforest,' said Malika.

Lizzie scowled at her, then stared fixedly down at the small black puddles forming in the mud. She was dimly aware of the two teenagers walking a short distance away from her before they stopped and began to talk. She felt full of charge, a violent, repellent terror. A terror that was worse than anything else she'd ever felt before because it was a terror of something she realised she could never get away from – *herself.*

'...hex...?' she heard Malika whisper, to which Zuri replied: 'Yes.'

But they might as well have been in a different world as she continued to stare at the glassy surfaces of the micro-puddles, bouncing and shaking in the rain. She let go of her ankle and put her arms around her knees, hugged them up against her chest.

After a while of listening to the hollow snapping of the rain and watching the puddles she became aware of another noise, a kind of crackling sound. Zuri and Malika were still talking, but she couldn't be bothered to listen to what they were saying. *But what was that other noise?* she wondered fleetingly, before disappearing into another far-off world of thought.

161

'Lizzie!'

Malika gripped her arm.

'We have to move!'

'What,' she said, looking up vacantly, then resentfully, at the girl.

'There's something coming,' said Zuri. She noticed how keenly he was scanning the forest behind them.

'What is it?' she said.

'I don't know, but we have to go,' said Zuri. 'Run – quickly – now!'

She felt herself pulled up by one on each side, and then she was back on her feet. Her ankle hurt, but it didn't give out on her. She looked back into the rain-pounded forest behind them. She could hear the sound louder now, the crackling had become a thrashing, as if something large was running towards them. The alarm felt by Zuri and Malika transferred to her, blotting out at least for the moment her dreadful meltdown.

And then the three teenagers were running, as fast as they could through the forest, away from whatever it was that was pursuing them.

Chapter 18: Battling The Demon

Very soon the ground began to rise which slowed their pace.

Scrambling over the slippery bark of a fallen tree, a few metres behind the others, Lizzie felt a sharp pain in her ankle and gasped. She stopped and looked back over her shoulder.

They had ascended more than she realised, as she was now just above the canopy of the forest through which they'd been trekking. As she looked, she saw a pair of brightly coloured birds – parrots or perhaps parakeets – rise up from the tree tops beneath her, emitting high pitched tweets. *They're frightened,* she thought. She knew she was going to have to keep running, regardless of the shooting pain in her ankle. She hoped it would hold out.

Then, just as she was turning to catch up with the others, the cracking and thumping sound became even louder and she caught sight of the creepers about ten metres away shaking. She knew she should have run then. But something made her stop.

She had a strange sense of déjà vu, of having been here before. She froze, waiting to see what would come out of the bushes, what had been pursuing them.

And somehow almost knowing what it was, but hoping desperately she was wrong.

In the next moment, the creepers flailed sideways and a monster broke free from the forest's tangle.

It was a bulky, man-sized creature, with a heavy brow and a large jaw filled with sharp, twisted teeth. Dark matted hair streamed back from the top of its blistered head, catching against the cloak that flew up from its back. The creature's hands ended in giant talons instead of fingers. In the amorphous lump of its face the eyes were incongruous, beady and small.

But, even at a distance, Lizzie knew they were not small eyes. They were the same human-sized eyes as the creature's alter ego. *Lady Eva Blane.*

'You!' she gasped – or at least she might have. Everything about the world seemed to have taken on an otherworldly, filtered light, and stood still.

The Pisaca stopped running. Lizzie could hear the noise of her breathing, loud and nasal and ill-designed, like a pug dog. Amidst the torrential rain, Lizzie could see steam rising off her.

Standing like that, staring across the open jungle at the Pisaca of Kashi, the strange anxiety and fear that Lizzie had just been absorbed by melted away. Oddly, she was no longer scared of her situation, and of herself. And even more oddly, she was not scared of the demon standing before her.

She was angry.

'It was you,' she said, semi-audibly, although of course the Pisaca with her special powers could easily hear her. 'It was you, right?' Everything was falling into place. 'You remembered our talk on the horses in Hebley and you used –' she swallowed, feeling rage engulf her '– you used all my suffering about my dad's death to try and break me. You used it...'

The Pisaca stood, her head tilted down but her eyes fixed on Lizzie. She was making short, erratic bovine snorts.

'So how come you're back?' said Lizzie, turning fully to face her. 'I thought we'd got rid of you for good that night on the ghats. What are you after this time?'

She began to walk back towards the demon.

'Has the cat got your tongue, Eva? You are Eva, aren't you? Or have I got it wrong? Perhaps you're one of the crazy cousins come down from the attic?'

The rain was streaming down her head, running into her eyes. But the world was bright, vivid.

She was walking towards a demon, taunting her as she went. *She had never felt so alive.*

'Come on, Eva, say something, you stupid, despicable piece of...'

And then the demon charged.

Despite her size, she came like a bolt of black lightning towards her. The peculiar, giddy high that Lizzie had felt instantly evaporated and she realised the mortal danger she was in. She screamed on the top of her voice and felt her legs buckling beneath her – although somehow she remained upright.

Eva was going to kill her.

Everything then happened so fast, almost too fast for her to comprehend. Suddenly someone was leaping past her, in front of her, skidding to a halt in the mud right in front of her and pulling something off his back, like a man pulling an arrow from a quiver.

It was Zuri!

The teenage boy was standing in the way, blocking the demon from coming on to her. The Pisaca came to a halt, a few steps before the young African hunter and shaman.

And then for the first time the demon spoke.

'Get out of my way,' she said, in her rough, gravelly voice.

'Whatever you are,' said Zuri, 'you cannot have her.'

He had put the Nkisi on the ground, and Lizzie noticed him now placing a nail on the top of the statue's head, raising a stone in his other hand.

Suddenly, Eva must have recognised what the boy had set down before her. 'That!' she cried. 'Give me that!'

'No!' shouted Zuri.

She began to run at the boy. He lifted his hand holding the rock high in the rain, then swung it down on top of the nail.

The mighty crack made the demon stop.

Everyone looked at the statue. And then the rain flashed, there was an odd sensation in Lizzie's ears as if the pressure had changed, and then the shimmering form of the Spirit Man sprang from the old nailed post into the wet reality of the jungle. Lizzie gasped, and raised a hand to her cheek as the man gave some kind of warped

166

shriek and ran like a gushing river straight into the stunned Pisaca.

The Spirit Man seemed to overwhelm her, taking her off guard and knocking her backwards on to the ground. Lizzie and Zuri watched as the two engaged in what was evidently some kind of part-physical, part-spiritual battle. At moments Eva almost looked as if she was fighting herself, as the Spirit Man seemed to fizz and briefly disappear, like a hologram, something experiencing weak electrical reception. But what was clear was the desperation in her fighting, the massive challenge this creature from another world posed for her. The Pisaca grunted and snorted as she battled for her life, and once even gave a very ladylike cry of anguish, in the exact same tone as Lady Blane of Hebley.

'What is it...?'

Lizzie realised that Malika had come up behind her, watching the surreal battle unfold.

'She's the Pisaca of Kashi,' said Lizzie. 'Lady Eva Blane...'

'*She?* It's a woman? And you *know* her?'

'We have to go – now!' said Zuri, interrupting them. 'I don't know how much power he has after we invoked him yesterday. And I don't know what he can do against something like *that*.'

With one final look at the surreal battling creatures, Lizzie and her companions turned and fled away up the hill, on towards the bandits and Thomas Bennett.

Chapter 19: The Ghost Boy in Hell

Thomas Bennett knew not to argue now when the one called Joseph handed him more of the disgusting slop. Instead he just drank it straight from the flask, trying to ignore the alien, slightly rancid flavour. *Like vinegary tomato juice, with horrible doughy lumps.*

Last time he had been offered it he'd tried to push it away and received a sharp cuff to the head. His ear was still sore from it. He'd even been worried that Joseph was going to strike him with the butt of his gun.

It was better just to eat, and do what he was told, when he was told to do it.

As he sat there, gagging on the gruel, sitting on a rock in the pouring rain in the midst of the jungle, surrounded by African men with dreadlocks and guns and odd, mainly western clothes, he found himself once again thinking about the Feral Child in Hebley.

The *Wild Boy of the Woods*.

Thomas realised now that all this – the discovery of the mask, the disappearance of the garden and its replacement by the mud-hut village and all those crazy men, his grabbing of the iron-spike club and flight into the trees – all this, plus the capture by these terrifying

168

bandits, the never-ending ordeal – was just some kind of sick joke, it was Fate playing a horrible joke on him because of the things he'd said and thought about that Wild Boy.

Seeing that Joseph had walked off and left him on his own, he allowed himself to mutter a few words aloud again. Hearing his own voice somehow helped continue the numbness – the numbness he needed more than anything after the constant panic and hysteria that had been his life for these past few days that felt like years.

'It was like this for you, wasn't it, hiding in the frozen woods, with your mum and dad dead and nothing to eat, nowhere to sleep but in the snow, it was so cold at night wasn't it, lucky you had Charlie Fox and Jenny Deer to help you, wasn't it, Charlie bringing you those rabbits to eat, and Jenny keeping you warm in the night against her nice furry tummy...'

He kind of knew that he'd made it all up, but the story was the only thing that gave him any reassurance now. It was too hard to think of anyone real, his mum or dad or even someone like Lizzie Jones whose garden he'd gone into. At first, when he was dragged along through the mud by the thugs he'd screamed for his mum, but soon he'd stopped, not because of the rough treatment but because it was just too hard – *far too hard* – to even think of his mum and home here, now.

No, he'd realised that the acutest part of this hell, the thing that made it so completely terrifying and tortuous, was not the pain caused by the devils who lived here – bad as that was – but the fact that it made your previous life, the memories of your loved ones, too painful to even think about. So you had to make the most terrible choice of all – to consciously forget about everyone you ever loved.

Better to think about the poor little gypsy boy lost in the snowy woods, with only his kind animal friends there to help him.

'Hey, Thomas, yo' finish yo' drink? Time to move now, again!'

It was Franck, the kindest of the kidnappers, a man with short curly grey hair who was always smiling at Thomas and who despite his rifle and machete Thomas was starting to think of as his only friend. True, Franck had been the one who shot that other man at point blank range shortly after they'd captured Thomas – but he wasn't creepy like Dudu or irritating like Bedel with his shrill high-pitched snigger, or just plain crazy like Joseph in his Bob Marley T-shirt. No, if he put the shooting out of his mind he could almost think of Franck as his friend. *Almost.*

Franck helped him to stand up, and even put an arm around his shoulder as he wretched up the little gruel he'd managed to swallow.

Then Thomas continued on into the tropical hell with the band of madmen.

Up ahead, through the trees, there soon grew a terrific crashing noise.

*

They fled up and down hills, through tangled thickets and across slippery rocks, until Lizzie and Malika could run no more.

170

And then they stopped.

Lizzie fell on to her knees, her forehead pressed against her crossed arms on the ground. For a good while all she could do was breathe, great big shuddering breaths, interspersed with the occasional fit of coughing.

Eva Blane was alive! She could barely comprehend it.

When her breathing calmed down, she looked up at her companions.

Zuri was standing above her, looking around at the tree tops and sky, taking in stuff like he always did. Unlike her and Malika, who was just pushing herself up into a sitting position, he didn't even look like he'd been running.

'How... how long do you think... the Spirit Man will hold her off?' she gasped.

Zuri shrugged.

'Impossible to say,' he said.

'Do you think he can kill her?' She couldn't even think what would happen if the Spirit Man wasn't able to defeat Eva. Then they were all dead, for sure. With the silence that greeted her from Zuri she realised the answer to her question: 'I know, I know – impossible to say...' she muttered.

'What are we going to do?' said Malika.

'Carry on as planned,' said Zuri. He reached over and touched the Nkisi stick in his pack. 'I will know when – or if – the Spirit Man returns.'

'Which way are the bandits?'

'That way,' said Zuri, pointing along the valley. 'And I think I know where they're going.'

171

They carried on walking throughout the afternoon.

The rain dried up – *thankfully* – and the looming threat of the demon reappearing receded as the sun came out and everything became hot and humid again. Left alone to her thoughts, Lizzie tried to process all the things that had happened in the last couple of days.

Oddly, she thought first about the appearance of Caroline when Zuri had first used the power of the Nkisi. Caroline had been in astral form, like the *ghost girl* she'd first seen out on the Louisianan swamp. What was the significance of that? And what was it she had said to her?

We are gone, Lizzie. It is you they need now. Take care, my friend, take care.

She remembered the words exactly, like they were script for her to read at the front of her mind.

But what had they meant? Who was the *we* she referred to? Was it Caroline and Lizzie, or Caroline and someone else? Another 'witchkin' as Ashlyn had called them both?

Where were they gone? And who was the *they* she talked about that needed her?

Obviously from the last bit about *taking care*, it was clearly not good news. She didn't like the edgy Louisianan girl when she first got stranded with her in Cypress House, but after all the mysteries had been unravelled and Mr Paterson was dead they had quickly become friends when Caroline had made a few clandestine visits to her garden.

She hoped nothing bad had happened to her.

Then Lizzie thought about the harder thing, the vision of her dad with his assistant Jane.

How could Eva do that? She realised now that everything Eva had ever said to her was simply a betrayal, an attempt to find out about the Lingam that she'd wanted so much. She might be able to assume human form, but whatever humanity she might once have possessed had long since vanished.

Lizzie wondered how the demon had managed to return. Perhaps the contact with the Lingam had only transported her somewhere else? Perhaps to the place demons normally lived, some part of the Astral Plane. Lizzie thought about her feverish trance, the searing place she'd seen when the Spirit Man had saved her. If that was the case, Eva had either found a way to get back herself – or someone else had helped her.

That thought was truly chilling. If the Lingam couldn't do it, would they ever be able to kill her? And what if Eva – and her companions, if there were any left – succeeded in getting the Artefacts Xing had talked about, and used them to stay on Earth forever? It didn't bear thinking about. So... *she wouldn't.*

How about that for a solution?

The Pisaca had almost – *almost* – succeeded in making her lose her mind with her nasty magic and hexes. But now Lizzie was going to do the only thing she knew she could to stay sane.

She was going to put everything out of her mind, except the task in hand. She would ignore Eva Blane and all the other terrible threats around, and just carry on putting one foot in front of the other.

And somehow, walking through the bright, rain-washed jungle plants in the afternoon sun, she managed a secret smile.

Chapter 20: Witness to the Slaughter

As soon as the twin gothic spikes of the Cypress House roof appeared between the trees, Ashlyn Williams knew that something was wrong.

She vaulted over the boundary fence and then noticed that the front door was half open – but no one was on the porch. There was no sign of Miles' customary whiskey on the little table or stool. The hush was too much, the emptiness too full. *Her sixth sense went into overdrive.*

For a moment, she wished she'd brought Madeline with her. Everything had been so crazy for the last few days, what with the disappearance of first Thomas and then Lizzie. It had been impossible to move through the village without stumbling across reporters and film crews. She felt so sorry for Lizzie's mum and Mrs Bennett, seeing them make their tear-streaked statements on TV. She and the other coven members had all joined in the police hunt, and she and Madeline had used their familiars, Lugh, her fox, and Madeline's crow, Elba, to try and find traces of them – but to no avail. So she had slipped around the police and the reporters who seemed to be constantly stationed around Rowan Cottage, and

175

begun a search through the garden tirthas. First she had gone to Kashi where she'd met Pandu and Raj, and then the Master of the Nets garden, where she'd spoken to Xing. All had agreed to hunt for Lizzie, but no one had had any luck.

After toying with the idea for a while, she had decided *not* to ask Madeline to help her search through the tirthas. Madeline had already been a great help in her research about Lizzie's relatives, giving her the link to Nancy in the old people's home in Ledbury – but now the old Wiccan was getting increasingly cantankerous, worried about her age, and they seemed to spend more and more of their time together arguing. *Especially now Madeline had had the impractical idea of using coven magic to heal her early stage leukaemia.* So Ashlyn had come alone on this trip to alert Caroline and Miles to Lizzie's disappearance.

Now, with a pack full of wet clothes on her back, she stopped and looked over the large villa, scanning the sash windows of the upstairs and downstairs – but she couldn't see any movement. She walked up to the porch steps and carefully climbed them, trying not to make any noise. At the front door she considered shouting *hello*, but her instincts held her back.

Something was wrong. *She was sure of it.*

She stepped slowly around the door, careful not to budge it, on to the soft red carpet of the hallway.

Inside, the house was absolutely still. The door at the end of the hall into the lounge was open and she began to walk slowly towards it, hoping no floorboards would creak and give her away.

She was half way down the corridor when she heard a thud from upstairs.

She turned and, once again suppressing an instinct to shout, hurried to the foot of the staircase.

She was just in time to see someone turning back from the top of the stairs, and fleeing away down the landing. Without stopping to think, she bounded up the stairs in pursuit.

When she reached the landing there was no sign of the intruder.

Slowly, she began to walk down the corridor, checking to see if any of the doors ahead were open. Halfway down, she spotted one that was ajar, with light streaming on to the landing carpet through the gap.

Holding her breath, she crept up to the door and craned her neck forward to peer through the gap.

She failed to stifle a gasp at the sight of someone's legs, toe-down against the floor.

Ashlyn snatched a vase from a small table in the hall and, raising it above her head, edged forward into the room.

The sight that met her felt like a cut to the heart.

The body she'd seen was Miles, face down on the floor with dark blood stains on his back, one arm stretched out over his head. Beside him – *no, no, even more impossible!* – was Caroline, lying on her back with her eyes closed, her beautiful blond hair spread about her face, a red spot like a poppy in the centre of her abdomen.

'No...' Ashlyn said, dropping to her knees to check for a pulse on the girl's neck. Even as she felt for the artery, she could see that the blood was dried and dark, not fresh at all. She could tell that the girl – *the darling, beautiful young girl, who had been through so much* – was dead. And now she saw that Miles' eyes were open, staring at the floor, lifeless.

'Oh, Mother...' she whispered.

A creak behind her made her twist and come up, snatching up the vase to defend herself.

The terrified boy had been hiding behind the door and was now trying to get back out on to the landing. Ashlyn sprang forward, and grabbed him around the tops of his arms. The two crashed heavily together on to the bedroom floor.

'Let me go!'

'No, I won't hurt you, Hector, it's me, Ashlyn! What happened?'

She felt his resistance vanish, and next thing they were both kneeling up looking into each other's faces. Ashlyn could see tears in his eyes.

'I'm sorry,' he said. 'I didn't do it, I found them like this...'

'You've got nothing to be sorry about, Hector,' said Ashlyn. 'I know it wasn't you. Was anyone else here?'

'No, no one. I came round a short while ago. The house was empty so I searched around. I found them here, but it wasn't me...'

'I know, I know,' said Ashlyn, forcing herself to stay calm.

'I reckon it was *him* – that weird English guy.'

'Who?'

'Mr Brown – Raymond Brown.'

'Who's that?'

'He said he was a tourist, a birdwatcher, staying in Labouchelle, and he got lost on the swamp in the storm. They let him stay the night...'

'An Englishman?'

'Yes, we were spying on him out at the lagoon, me and Caroline, we heard him on the phone, then he must have heard us so I came out of cover and made a diversion while Caroline got away. I went home then came back this morning to see what had happened and...'

He stopped talking as sobs overtook him.

Ashlyn pulled him close to her and held him tight. All the while she was looking over his shoulder, at the body of Caroline. It was hard not to believe that the girl wouldn't just wake up any moment, prove that she wasn't really dead. Tears slipped down her cheeks as she tried to maintain a grip, a horrendous, ominous feeling bearing down on her.

'What did the man look like?' she said.

'Tall. With grey – or kind of silver – hair, and glasses.'

An image appeared in her head. 'What was he wearing?'

'A check jacket – with a white shirt. He was pretty smart. Except for the boots, because he'd been on the bayou.'

'When he arrived at the house – do you know if he was wet?'

'Wet? I don't know. But he came in the night, during the crazy storm. So I suppose he was wet.'

A good excuse, thought Ashlyn. She was sure it was *him*. The one she and Lizzie were certain was involved with the conspiracy to get the Artefacts, Eva Blane's confidante in the village.

The fox hunter, Godwin Lennox.

He was a murderer.

Then another thought struck her like ice down the spine.

Where was the Hilili Kachina doll?

*

The three teenagers pushed on through the jungle, half terrified of being caught up by the Pisaca from behind, half terrified of stumbling on the bandits ahead.

For an hour or so they said nothing to each other, each deep in the shadow of their own thoughts. The sun started to sink towards the mountains in the west, turning the sky a lovely peach and mauve, with bright clouds shredded along the peaks. Way down below where they trudged, the forest began to fade into murk.

'I'm starving,' said Malika.

Zuri stopped and looked around at the darkening trees. 'I would like to carry on,' he said, looking at the wretched, crumpled expressions on the girls' faces. 'But I think we're going to have to risk camping again.'

'We can go on,' said Lizzie half-heartedly.

'Malika's head is still bruised, and you're limping from your ankle,' said Zuri. 'Let's stop. Here is fine, we can build a fire.'

So they pegged up their makeshift tarpaulin between four small trees, and fixed their hammocks beneath it.

Zuri then made a small fire and they ate the last remaining avocado and bananas.

'We'll catch them tomorrow,' said Zuri, as they sat and watched sparks fly up from the fire. In the darkness around them, Lizzie heard the whirring of the crickets, which would have been lulling if it weren't for the constant interruptions of croaking frogs and squawking birds.

'Do we have a plan for rescuing the Ghost Boy?' said Malika.

For the first time, Lizzie detected a sardonic edge to her voice. She looked at the brother and sister, who had gone silent again and were staring solemnly into the orangey flames. She thought again just how beautiful they both were. *Living perfections.*

'Look, I... I'm really sorry I got you into all this,' she said. 'I know you've given up everything you care about to carry on with me. And... and that none of this would have happened if Thomas hadn't turned up. And without that stupid tirtha...'

Zuri looked at her. 'The tirtha is not your responsibility,' he said. 'And if it weren't for the magic of that portal, we would never have known your great-uncle. Where would be now without him?'

'Probably kicked out of the village,' said Malika. 'Way you used to wind everyone up. Especially Salomon....'

For the first time, Lizzie saw Zuri smile.

'Hey,' said Malika, 'remember that time you dug a hole outside his door?'

181

'I only wanted to trip him up when he got home in the dark.'

'Yes – look what happened!'

'I never knew his TV was getting delivered that day. How could I have known that?'

'*First* TV in the village!'

'What happened?' said Lizzie.

'Imagine!' said Malika. 'Two men arriving after dark, carrying this huge TV between them. They'd already carried it three miles together, through the jungle, from the road where their van got stuck....'

'There was Salomon, running round all excited like this baby warthog, showing them the way to the house,' said Zuri.

'The first one missed it,' said Malika. 'But the second guy's foot went down the hole...'

'I remember the noise,' said Zuri.

'The sound of it cracking? The whole screen was smashed,' said Malika. 'I've never seen anyone so boiling mad as Salomon that night!'

'Did he know it was you?' said Lizzie.

'Of course he did,' said Malika. 'No one else would dare do something like that!'

'What did he do?'

'It ran and ran,' said Malika. 'He made everyone in the whole village suffer for weeks.'

'I got the worst of it,' said Zuri. 'He gave me a real beating!'

'Quite right, too,' said Malika.

Lizzie thought back to her great-uncle's journal entries about the village, and particularly about Zuri. She had got the strong impression from them that he was just this crazy, out-of-control kid. *Which it sounded like he was.* But from Malika's chuckling, she now saw there must have been something... *endearing* about his mischief too. And on top of that there was his shamanism, his trips into the spirit world, as well as his amazing hunting skills. No doubt about it, Zuri was one of the most mysterious – and *interesting* – people she'd ever met.

The two siblings continued reminiscing about Zuri's juvenile pranks and exploits, with Lizzie alternately amazed, shocked, and laughing along. When they finally grew quiet, after a few moments Malika said:

'No, girl, you don't have to be sorry for anything. It's all part of *life's rich pageant*, isn't that what they say?'

Lizzie smiled. 'Thank you,' she said. 'Thank you both so much.' And then she added, because it was true: 'I would be dead if I hadn't met you two.'

'Still plenty of time for that,' said Zuri.

After sitting looking at the fire for a little longer, they all climbed into their hammocks and were soon fast asleep.

*

Lizzie woke up to the delicious smell of cooking meat.

It was still very dark in the forest, so she marvelled at how Zuri had managed to find and catch something for their breakfast. But when she climbed out of her hammock and approached the fire she recoiled from the sight of the long, white stringy creature he'd spitted on a makeshift twig fork.

'Tell me that's not a snake?' she said.

'Didn't even have to go looking for him,' he said. 'Found him right here, asleep by the fire.'

'I'm not touching it!' she said.

'Ever eat chicken?' said Malika, coming over. She yawned, scratching her tousled hair.

'You've got to be kidding,' said Lizzie, spotting what she first thought was a belt beside the fire but which she soon realised was the snake's *skin*.

But in the end she realised she was so hungry and she'd managed to put so many other things out of her mind that the least she could do was try it.

'What about the poison?' she said, tentatively taking a small bite.

'We're not eating the head,' said Zuri.

After the first mouthful, Lizzie realised it was delicious, and crammed as much as she could get down.

Then they packed up in the early light, and set off along a narrow trail following an incline uphill.

After an hour or so they stopped and turned back to watch the sun coming up over the jungle canopy below them, shimmering in the early morning haze. As its first rays lit the treetops with soft gold-green light, Lizzie wondered if across all her travels through the tirthas she'd ever seen anything quite so beautiful. Despite the hardships, she realised she was starting to love the jungle, and the people she had met here.

What a turnaround, she thought.

184

They finished off the remains of the cooked snake as a snack, and carried on. After a short while, Lizzie began to hear a rustling sound ahead.

'Is that a river?' she said.

Zuri nodded. 'The same one we were paddling on two days ago. We're near where it comes out of the mountains. It takes a very wide curve through that valley before eventually sweeping back to where we were on it.'

When they finally reached the river, it was a much clearer, faster running stretch than the one they had paddled on. Zuri was now following the trail of the kidnappers with ease, as they were sticking close to the river bank.

Shortly before midday, the noise of the water began to grow louder for no apparent reason. Lizzie was confused.

'Why's it getting louder?' she said.

'You'll see,' said Zuri.

And sure enough, after a few hundred metres, they broke through a dense thicket of vines and creepers and found themselves coming out on to a stone ledge before a large pool sculpted from the rocks. Feeding the pool was the tallest, most magnificent waterfall Lizzie had ever seen.

'Wow...' she gasped, gazing up at the masses and masses of water tumbling from a ledge high above them, a rainbow sheen at its sunny edge.

'*La Cascade de Rêveur*,' said Malika.

'Yes,' said Zuri. 'The Dreamer Falls...'

Chapter 21: To the Edge

'Get down!'

Without thinking, Lizzie obeyed Zuri's command and ducked down behind the rock.

'What is it?'

'I just saw them, halfway up the waterfall trail,' he said. 'If one of them looked down he'd see us.'

They sat with their backs against the damp stone, Zuri occasionally peeping over the top to check on the bandits' progress. Just over an hour later the men with Thomas reached the top and disappeared out of sight. The teenagers emerged to stand at the edge of the large, crashing pool that flowed away at its far edge as the mighty river.

'Look – a boat!' said Malika.

Lizzie looked where she was pointing and saw a small brown canoe, pulled up out of the pool just to one side of the waterfall.

'Must be one of theirs,' said Zuri.

Lizzie stared up at the bright white and silver gossamer of the falls above them. The water had a strange, contradictory quality, full of surging, restless power but also somehow especially round the edges almost drifting and weightless. But its sound was

186

consistent and deafening, as if there was too much of it for the air to hold, a pent-up pressure in the inner ear. Lizzie imagined how quickly she'd be lost if she went anywhere near that torrent of spray and froth. It was like a mighty monster, something immortal and divine from the start of the world, totally absorbed in its own mystery. She felt miniscule and in awe, both at the same time.

'Come on,' said Zuri. 'We can go up now.'

They followed the zigzagging path up the side of the falls, which soon narrowed and began to climb steeply, the drop to their side becoming treacherous. The rocks glistened with a fine sheen of water from the spray, but Lizzie was sure footed and didn't have too much of a problem with heights, just as long as she didn't spend too much time looking down. But at one stage she heard a crackle of pebbles giving way behind her and looked over her shoulder to see Malika frowning and leaning with her back pressed against the rock face.

'You OK?' she shouted, against the tumult of the water.

'Yes!' said the girl, but clearly she wasn't.

'Hold on to my hand.'

'But then we'll both go if I fall.'

'No we won't. I'll stop you.'

They carried on climbing in the roasting heat of the midday sun. At one stage, where the path broadened at its furthest point from the falls, Zuri stopped and suggested they drink. They perched themselves on a low rock, looking down at the sweep of the jungle hundreds of feet below them. *Like one great big broccoli forest*, thought Lizzie.

'There's a good space to camp near the top of the falls,' said Zuri. 'My guess is they will stop there. A few miles upstream there's a large village, with a good phone mast. I think they've been heading here to get reception to make their ransom demand, well away from where they think Thomas' parents are.'

'If only they knew the truth,' said Lizzie. 'Couldn't they just have called from anywhere in the jungle?'

'No, most of it has no signal. Even where there should be, the wet canopy is good at blocking it,' said Zuri.

Lizzie wondered what Thomas' parents would do if they suddenly got a call telling them their son was kidnapped and in the middle of Africa.

Can't think about that now, she told herself. *There's a job to do.*

Although, of course, she hadn't got a clue how they were going to do it.

*

After another hour of climbing they stopped again, a short distance from what Lizzie reckoned was the top – although she'd thought that before and now realised the top was never where you thought it was when you were climbing. She turned and looked across the bright, frothy water of the falls, fanning outwards as it fell from the lip of rock above. She imagined the millions of gallons of water disappearing over that edge every single day, year in year out.

'I'll go up first and check it out,' said Zuri to the girls.

'But they'll see you,' said Lizzie.

'Probably not,' said Zuri. 'They're not expecting to be followed anymore – they'll probably be settling down for the night.'

'OK,' said Lizzie. She put her arm around Malika's shoulder and leaned with her back into the rockface.

She watched as Zuri climbed up and quickly disappeared from sight. Malika looked miserable.

'We'll be all right,' said Lizzie.

Malika nodded.

Hardly a minute passed before the boy was back again.

'I was right,' he said. 'They've set up camp near the top. And the path forks up there so we can follow it into the forest and get a good look at what they're doing. We can make a plan before nightfall.'

'OK,' said Lizzie.

They scrambled up the final stretch, their thoughts growing increasingly dark as they fully absorbed the challenge that lay ahead of them.

And, as they climbed, not one of them threw a final glance back at the mesmerising cascade of the Dreamer Falls; not one of them looked at the magnificent rainforest glowing in the late afternoon sun, stretching hundreds of miles away beneath them; so not one of them saw Eva Blane, the Pisaca of Kashi, as she stepped boldly out from the jungle on to the soaking rocks below, and turned her grotesque head up towards them.

Chapter 22: In The Bandit Camp

'What do you think he's doing?'

'I don't know,' said Zuri suspiciously. 'I think he's just going to see if he can shoot some bushmeat for dinner. But I'm not sure.'

They were crouching in a bush looking across a grassy knoll to where the bandits were setting up their camp. One of them, an older looking man with short hair, was wandering away from the group into the dark wall of trees, rifle in hand.

'So what *is* the plan?' said Malika, more serious this time.

'We wait until they've settled down for the night, and hope that the lookout falls asleep again,' said Zuri. 'Then we creep in, grab Thomas, and get out again.'

'You make it all sound so easy,' said Lizzie.

'What then?' said Malika.

'Down the path again. And we use that boat to get him away as fast as possible. There's no way they'll catch us if we're on the river.'

'I hadn't thought of that!' said Lizzie, momentarily excited before her hope was once more crushed by the likelihood of them succeeding in getting Thomas out in the first place. These guys had *guns*.

'Yes, it shouldn't take much more than a day, day-and-a-half, to get back. It's all downstream, and fast,' said Zuri.

They were so near – and yet so far.

Lizzie watched the men carefully for a while. One of them, the guy with the dreadlocks and Bob Marley T-shirt, was speaking to Thomas, who was sat looking wretched with his back hunched by the fire. They were much too far away for her to hear what he was saying. After a moment, the man suddenly clubbed Thomas round the top of the head with his gun, causing the boy to scream out. Then he grabbed Thomas' shirt, hauled him up, and led him over to the largest tent in the centre of the camp. He lifted the flap, and shoved the boy inside.

'What shall...' began Lizzie, when an unexpected sound, *a cough*, came from behind them.

Spinning round, she found herself looking down the barrel of a rifle, held by the grey haired man.

'*Venez avec moi*,' he said.

The three teenagers stood slowly, raising their hands up above their heads in the universal sign of surrender.

*

'I'm sure it was Godwin Lennox!'

In her small cottage in the woods on the far side of Hebley, Ashlyn Williams was talking to her elderly Wiccan friend, Madeline Kendall. Outside an owl hooted in the warm summer evening.

'Hector's description of him was spot on,' Ashlyn continued. 'And he never replied to any of Rachel's phone calls.'

'But he was with the Assistant Chief Constable, Jim Weston, all the time,' said Madeline. 'Jim put out a statement about it as soon as they got back from their shooting break and heard about the rumours. They didn't have any signal in the place they were staying, and Godwin had told Rachel that's what he was doing.'

'I know,' said Ashlyn. 'But I don't trust Jim an inch, either. He was always over at Eva's, at this party or that. I'm sure he's either in with them, or they've bought him off. Poor Rachel, what must she be going through...' She thought about how the papers and social media were unfolding their partial glimpses of the story hour by hour.

'Ashlyn, I... I saw Godwin with Jim.'

'You saw him? What were you doing? Joining them on their shooting break?'

'Of course not! I passed them on the road on my way to Ledbury. They were in Jim's old Land Rover.'

'How can you be sure it was them?'

'It was the dogs in the back that gave it away. All those beagles.'

Ashlyn snatched her wine off the coffee table and sunk back into the sofa.

'I feel so depressed, powerless.'

'We've done everything we possibly can now,' said Madeline. 'Raj and Pandu are searching the ghats, speaking to people about whether they've seen Lizzie –

or Thomas – and Xing has been looking too. We just have to wait. Lizzie – and Thomas – will turn up, I'm sure.'

'Yes, yes, and what happened in Cypress House will just go down as another sad result of America's crazy gun obsession. Some freak hillbilly burglar breaking in and gunning down the owners...'

'You got Hector to get his dad to help him report it to the Sheriff,' said Madeline. 'And the men round the lagoon – all of them who Paterson made into plat eyes – know about the possibility of someone coming through the tirtha, so they're on their guard. There's nothing more we can do.'

'It's so frustrating. Without the police knowing about the tirthas, that whole aspect of the investigation falls on us. We're not detectives!'

'We will do what we can,' said Madeline. 'We can do no more.'

'With all we've found out from your cousin, Nancy, I'm sure Lizzie's connection with Hattie has something to do with all this,' said Ashlyn.

'Who knows,' said Madeline. 'Try not to worry.'

Ashlyn looked at her wine glass and sighed. 'I just... I just *wish Eric was still alive*,' she said. 'He would know what to do.'

∗

'So what we goin' t'do wi' the three *petits enfants*?'
'Put 'em on the fire and eat 'em for tea!'

Lizzie felt her skin crawl as the skinny man whose idea it was to eat them emitted a strange, high-pitched giggle. *Who were these people?* What were they capable of?

She glanced uncertainly across at Malika and Zuri. They were all now sitting in the centre of the camp by a new fire, all looking up at the barrels of the various guns directed at them.

'We've got to be worth more than that to you,' said Malika.

'You's worth a lot t'me, honey,' said another one of the men, with short corkscrew hair and an unbuttoned red-check shirt. Several others broke into laughter, and snorted with approval and excitement.

'Stop!' It was the man with dreadlocks and the Bob Marley T-shirt. 'There's somethin' don't add up 'bout all this. What are these kids doin' followin' us through the jungle?'

'You stole our Nkisi,' said Zuri.

'And my... *friend*,' said Lizzie.

'Yes, an' I'm taking it back right now,' said the man, stepping forward and pulling the Nkisi out of Zuri's backpack with two quick tugs. Zuri fumed, but did nothing to stop him.

'What about yo' parents?' said the man. 'Where's they?'

'They said we had to wait for your call,' said Malika.

'But we had other ideas,' said Zuri.

'You are making a call, aren't you?' said Lizzie.

'Shut up!'

They all froze in the face of the man's sudden ferocity.

'Do you think I'm stupid?'

They kept quiet.

'Put 'em in the tent with their friend,' he said. 'While I work out what we goin' t' do wi' 'em.'

The older one, whose name they'd heard as Franck, led them over at rifle-point to the large tent. He raised the flap and gestured for them to go inside. Lizzie came last, her panic temporarily disappearing as she realised she was on the verge of seeing Thomas again.

'*Hurrhh!*'

The English boy fell backwards in surprise and terror as the three teenagers crowded in on top of him.

'Thomas!' She pushed past Zuri and Malika – *there was scarcely room for anyone in this tent!* – and grabbed the boy's hands. 'Thomas, it's me!'

'What are *you* doing here?'

'Thomas, I'm here to help!'

Lizzie looked into his eyes, and saw they were still wild, unable to cope with the situation. He had a nasty congealed cut on the top of his head, where the man with dreads had struck him.

'There's magic in the garden – real magic, Thomas! That mask you looked in, it transported you here. It's like something out of the movies, only real. I came through to find you!'

Suddenly, he was holding on to her, pressing his face into her shoulder, sobbing.

Lizzie held him tight, throwing a brief embarrassed glance at Zuri and Malika as they squatted on their haunches behind them.

'It's OK, Thomas, it's OK,' she said. 'It's been too much, I know. But we're going to help you.'

The boy didn't look up but, gripping her ever tighter around the arms and back, said: 'Don't go, you can't leave me. You've got to get me home...'

'I will – we will,' said Lizzie.

'Don't you dare go,' he said. 'You stay with me, get me back. Please, Lizzie…'

'I will,' she said again, briefly feeling a moment of indignation as if he were bating her about something back in Hebley, before it disappeared as she remembered all he'd been through. 'I will.'

'Thank you,' he mumbled.

And then, as if the memory of their year-long antipathy were somehow stronger than everything else they'd suffered in the last few days, he suddenly pulled back and they let each other go. They each looked away.

'Yes, well – no problems,' said Lizzie.

'No, no problems at all,' said Zuri, leaning forward so his narrow, handsome face was between them. 'Just as soon as we've figured out how to outwit seven gunmen and get the Nkisi back we'll be on our way. You'll be home in no time!'

'I don't have a...' began Lizzie, but then stopped as she heard a strange sound outside over the muffled boom of the falls. It was a low crunching sound, like a bag of rice hitting a hard floor and splitting.

'What was that?' she said, and the four teenagers all froze and listened.

The next thing Lizzie heard was a brief cry, and then the same strange sound, like something ripping, again.

'*Mon dieu!*' someone outside yelled.

And then there was a scream, a terrible, blood-curdling scream, and the shooting began.

Thomas gripped his ears and rocked forward as Lizzie pulled everyone together into a small huddle in the centre of the tent. They cringed, and blinked, and gasped as the guns carried on firing, like some shattering, staccato firework display.

'What's happening?' said Malika.

'Don't know,' said Zuri.

There was another cry, more shrill and *desperate* than the others, followed by a thump and then a sobbing cry of '*Maman, maman...*'.

A different gun, not one of the automatic AK-47 rifles, fired once, twice, and there was a pig-like snort and grunting.

'*Non...*' someone cried.

There was a final gunshot, then everything went quiet.

Lizzie looked up, straight into Zuri's dark eyes. A moment of comprehension passed between them.

'The Pisaca...' she whispered.

Zuri nodded.

He reached forward and slowly lifted up the tent flap.

197

Chapter 23: Falls

She knew she had to go too.

As soon as Zuri stepped out of the tent and stood up, Lizzie swallowed her fear and climbed out behind him.

She couldn't believe the scene before her.

Eva – *the Pisaca* – had massacred them. All seven men lay strewn around the campsite, their stomachs, faces, necks all torn and split. Blood, guts and brains oozed from corpses. Lizzie caught a brief glimpse of their leader, the man with the dreads, lying disembowelled with his arms stretched out towards his gun. She quickly looked away.

And found herself staring at the tall, handsome figure of Lady Eva Blane, a short distance away from them.

Eva was in her black cloak with her legs apart, her dark hair blowing around her shoulders in the breeze that was coming off the fast-flowing river. Standing near the edge of the cliff, in the soft evening light with the fine mist of the falls behind her, she looked like something out of a myth or legend.

Which, Lizzie thought, *technically she was.*

'Time to take you home, Lizzie,' said Eva.

This time, Lizzie decided she would ignore her. If she was going to die, she was going to abstain from all the silly talk.

It was then she noticed a slight movement in Zuri's arm. She glanced down and saw him drawing something from the frayed back pocket of his shorts. *A nail!*

She looked across to the fire, where the bandit leader had taken the Nkisi out of Zuri's pack. Sure enough, the decrepit-looking statue was still there, lying on the ground.

Would it work? Surely Eva had defeated the Spirit Man – otherwise she wouldn't even be here.

Well, there was little alternative but to try.

She heard a voice behind her.

'You go left, I'll go right. Get a gun.'

It was Malika, coming out of the tent behind her. Lizzie grasped the plan – all three of them would split up, with her and Malika heading out either side whilst Zuri ran straight ahead to the Nkisi – *and Eva* – in the hope he could activate the Artefact before Eva finished them all off.

Fat chance.

But, without any other options, and with Eva *right now* transforming back into the demon as she walked slowly towards them, Lizzie nodded.

'OK,' whispered Malika. 'Three, two, one... GO!'

Lizzie lost sight of the other two as she dashed off to the left. Out of the corner of her eye she glimpsed the Pisaca running forward, but couldn't be sure who the demon was heading for.

After a short sprint she reached the mutilated body of the bandit leader and snatched up his AK-47.

Or tried to – the thing weighed a ton! But after falling into a crouch she managed to lift it up and prop it on her knee. Then she looked up, half expecting to find the Pisaca crashing into her and shredding her into pieces.

But no, she saw that Eva was heading for Zuri, the obvious choice as her most strong and dangerous opponent. And thankfully something, perhaps her transformation, had slowed her down – *Lizzie fleetingly recalled the almost slow-motion way in which Eva had transformed in Rowan Cottage* – giving Zuri the precious few seconds he needed to reach the Nkisi. The boy had fallen on to his knees beside it, and was bringing up the nail and a pistol he had snatched up to use as a hammer.

Then Lizzie heard a bang, and another one, and saw the Pisaca shudder a little as she began to run forward. She looked over and saw that Malika had found a pistol too and was firing it off.

Lizzie wrestled with her own gun but quickly realised that she could barely lift it, let alone aim it well enough to ensure she didn't hit Zuri. So she dropped it, drew out her small pocket knife, and began to run towards the boy, like the Pisaca.

There was one more bang, which shook the Pisaca's head, and then Malika screamed like a bloodthirsty warrior and began to run forward too.

As she ran, Lizzie watched as the massive demon bore down on the crouching Zuri. Her mind a whirl of panic, desperate hope, and strange wonder, she saw his hand with the gun swing up and then come back down for a mighty blow. The crack on the nail was audible even above the tumultuous pounding of the waterfall.

For a moment Lizzie was dimly aware that everyone, including the Pisaca herself, had stopped, watching the ancient statue to see what happened.

When nothing did, the demon leapt forward and Lizzie shrieked in horror as Zuri disappeared with a cry beneath her mighty bulk. Lizzie's heart lifted briefly as she saw the boy's arms come out, his head come up for a second, pushing back at the demon as she pressed down on him – and then the Pisaca's claws came out and diced nimbly around his head and chest. The boy fell back to the ground, blood flowing from his many wounds.

'NO!' yelled Malika, flinging herself the last couple of feet into the demon, and somehow knocking the far larger monster sideways and off her brother.

Lizzie ran forward, watching as Eva regained her footing and righted herself, spit and blood whipping away from her fangs. The Pisaca roared and lunged at Malika who dived away to land on her face, narrowly avoiding her opponent's grasp.

As the demon swung round preparing to pounce on the girl's back, Lizzie finally came up behind her and, yelling at the top of her voice, struck her small knife into the creature's shoulder. The Pisaca didn't even notice as she leant over and lifted Malika up from the ground by her arms. Lizzie struck again and again, the small blade ripping through the black cloak each time and coming

201

back with a small amount of sticky grey-blue goo which she realised must be the demon's blood.

'Stop!' snarled the Pisaca throatily, and she swung Malika round in a circle to collide her with Lizzie.

Next thing Lizzie knew she was on the ground with Malika on top of her. Both girls turned to look up, to see the terrifying demon bearing down on them.

'No more keeping you alive,' hissed the Pisaca. 'I have another, after all…'

Realising there was nothing they could do, Lizzie and Malika threw their arms around each other and hugged tightly. Fleetingly, Lizzie wondered where Thomas was, but a quick glance at the tent showed that he didn't even appear to have come out.

This was it.

She held her breath and scrunched up her eyes as a taloned hand came slicing down towards the top of her head – only to be struck away by something else.

Lizzie looked up to see the Pisaca grasping her arm and roaring. And there, standing beside her, the Nkisi raised in both hands above his head, was Zuri!

The boy had long, terrible cuts down his face, his T-shirt was shredded in several places, and he had gashes down his arms – but he was alive! With a defiant cry, he brought the statue, now little more than a nailed club, down on to the skull of the Pisaca.

And, unlike all the bullets and the knife, it *did* cause her to bellow with rage and pain, the nails scoring gashes across her leathery forehead and cheek. Two small lumps of yellow flew from her mouth, *teeth*, Lizzie realised.

Before the demon could recover herself, Zuri had yelled and struck her twice more, once on the arm and the other time with a thrusting blow into the stomach. Eva stumbled back a few paces.

'The Spirit Man is gone but the statue still has power against her...' Lizzie said in awe.

'Dieu merci,' whispered Malika, and then she cried out as the Pisaca landed a swiping blow on Zuri and sent the boy staggering back towards them.

'Come on, we have to help him!' shouted Lizzie, and they both sprang up and charged forward.

But Zuri was back into the fray on his own, butting and striking the Pisaca with the Nkisi in a state of frenzy. The far larger creature was stumbling back with each blow, clearly feeling it for once. Briefly, Lizzie was reminded of the damage the Lingam did to her – at least when she touched it with her bare flesh. *Could the Nkisi be doing something similar?*

'Yes!' she screamed as she saw a spray of blood coming off the top of the demon's head, as Zuri landed a particularly good blow.

And then she gasped as the Pisaca lunged and seemed to catch hold of Zuri, making the boy stop his reckless attack, only a short distance from the mighty river and the cliff edge over which it disappeared.

Lizzie and Malika stopped together, in shock, just behind Zuri, witnessing the dark bloom of blood on the back of his yellow T-shirt. The Pisaca was looking down her stubby nose and giant jaws into his face as he looked up at her, grimacing with pain.

And then Lizzie realised the awful truth: *he was impaled on her claws.*

Zuri gasped in agony. With her free hand, the Pisaca prised the Nkisi out of his grip, clearly unaffected by touching it alone. Even with that atrocious, swollen face, Lizzie was sure that Eva was grinning.

Lizzie saw Zuri twisting up his face in the last desperate throes of agony and... and... something else. *Defiance.*

To Lizzie's astonishment, she saw the tall, handsome boy, the boy for whom she had felt, *felt* something, grit his teeth, and suddenly push – *push!* – the demon backwards with all his might.

And somehow Eva stumbled, her feet slipping on the rock, going back, back with the boy, closer and closer to the edge of the falls.

Eva's face contorted from surprise back into rage and she struck down on Zuri with the Nkisi, hitting him on the shoulder, ripping through cloth and flesh with the thick, rusty nails.

Zuri responded with a furious roar, and pushed her back further, his feet splayed to hold his ground, like a rugby player in a scrum.

By the time Eva realised exactly what the boy's plan was, it was too late.

Zuri had wrestled her back out on to a broad, featureless slab of rock, glistening wet from the spray of the falls over which it hung. Glancing over her shoulder, Eva saw how close the edge had come and for one moment her face registered something Lizzie had only seen on it once before: *terror.*

Desperately, the Pisaca struck the boy once more with the spiked statue, as he gave a final scream and shoved her over the roaring precipice.

Lizzie's eyes widened in awe and desperate hope as she saw the Pisaca flail backwards, her cloak and hair spreading out in the wind – *he'd done it, Zuri had done it!*

And then she wailed as Eva's hand somehow snatched the boy's arm and he disappeared from sight, pulled over the edge and into the Dreamer Falls with the Pisaca of Kashi.

Chapter 24: The Journey Back

Time stopped as the two girls stood there, on the rock overhanging the thundering falls, staring down at the pool hundreds of feet below, in the vague hope they would see him surface.

It began to get dark.

'He saved us,' said Lizzie, putting her arm around Malika's shoulder as the girl continued weeping silently. 'Come on. We have to stay here tonight.'

'But he might still be alive!'

Swallowing hard, Lizzie threw one more glance over the precipice. There was no way anyone could have survived that, she knew it. *But what could she say?*

'We can't go down tonight, we'd never survive the climb down in the dark,' she said.

'But I want to! Tomorrow will be too late! Suppose he's lying there on a rock, injured?'

'If we survived the climb down we'd have no chance of finding him in the dark,' said Lizzie. But she was even starting to doubt herself – perhaps they should risk everything just for that one in a million, one in a *billion*, chance they might find him alive – when Malika said:

'No. You're right. We must stay here. If we die by our rashness, he will have died in vain.'

Lizzie, who was doing everything she could to fight her overwhelming desire to wail and curl up in a little ball, nodded. Then, like two zombies, they walked back towards the camp fire, the only advantage of the darkness being that they didn't have to look at all the fresh corpses strewn around.

It was only then that Lizzie remembered.

'Thomas!' she cried, and ran to the tent, closely followed by Malika.

'Go away!' she heard him cry as she lifted the flap.

In the dim light from the distant fire, she could just make out his cringing shape at the back of the tent. Her sympathy evaporated.

'Come out, Thomas,' she said coldly.

'What about the men?'

'They're all dead.'

'Dead!'

'Yes. They were slaughtered by a demon. You remember Lady Blane? Not been seen in the village since last year? It was her. She was also killing lots of Indian kids, but we managed to stop her doing that. Only now...she's gone and killed Zuri...'

'Lizzie!' said Malika.

Lizzie turned away and marched back to the fire, tears streaming down her cheeks. *Why did he get to live – the little coward! – whilst Zuri was dead?*

She sat down by the fire, dimly aware that Malika and Thomas were talking, and stared into the rich yellow flames. A random thought crossed her mind – *what if Eva had survived the fall?* – before she dismissed it, thinking even if she had and came back for them there was nothing they could do this time. *No point in worrying about things you can't do anything about*, as her dad used to say.

Her dad...

Her mind went blank for an unknown period as she was taken over by the hypnotic flames.

'Lizzie.'

She felt a hand on her shoulder, looked up to see Malika offering her some water. She drank, wiped the wetness from her cheeks. She felt a momentary admiration for Malika, that her brother was lost, but still she found the will to continue. She looked across and saw Thomas sitting staring vacantly on the other side of the fire. She hadn't even noticed him sit down, didn't know how long he'd been there.

'Is there any food?' she asked.

'Yes,' said Malika. 'I've found some *kwanga* – dried bread – groundnuts and honey.'

Whilst Malika shared the food out, Lizzie looked at Thomas and said: 'I know you've been through a lot. We'll get you home soon.'

'Home?'

'Yes. There's a boat down below the falls. It will get us back to the tirtha – the magic portal – in a day or so. Then in a moment we'll be back in Hebley.'

She felt a glimmer of sympathy return when she saw him bow his head and begin to sob, overcome with emotion.

*

The next morning Lizzie was woken by a sudden bird shriek, before once more she became aware of the noise of the river and the falls.

They had all somehow managed to sleep in the tent, exhausted from their ordeal, careless of any other danger. Lizzie woke Malika and then Thomas, and they all went out into the violet, pre-dawn light.

Aware of the dead men, they decided to take their packs and head straight down the cliff path to the pool. They could eat there, once they had searched for Zuri.

As they descended the sun rose up above the horizon, bringing the jungle into crisp detail with its orangey hue. Stopping for a moment on the sheer path, listening to the cacophony of the falls, Lizzie felt a sudden burgeoning, as if there were too much feeling inside her: misery – *utter, ridiculous misery* – panic and loss, but also something different and strange, an incredible awe and yearning. Quickly, she looked away from the astonishing natural beauty and carried on, afraid that she might lose her grip on reality if she indulged such overpowering emotions.

An hour later they reached the bottom and began a slow and painful search around the large pool. After another hour they gave up, realising they were not going to find Zuri.

So they climbed into the boat and let the current take them rapidly downstream, initially only needing to paddle to keep themselves away from the rocks and riverbank.

Once they reached a slower, quieter stretch of river, they began to take it in turns to paddle properly. Taking one of the oars from Malika, Lizzie said to her:

'What are we going to say? I mean... how are we going to tell them?'

'I've been thinking about it,' said Malika. 'We should say he died fighting the bandits.'

'What about Eva?'

'She's dead now. If we talk about demons the right people won't believe us – and the wrong people will. It will cause mayhem – and fear – in the village for months, possibly years. The important thing is that we know...' she swallowed, her eyes filling with tears, '... the important thing is that *we* know the truth. We know what he did... we know how much of a hero he was.'

'What about your mum?'

'Her... I think I will tell her the truth. But not for a while.'

*

The journey downriver was fast and when darkness fell they were lucky to have a good waxing moon to see by so decided not to camp and instead pushed on through the night, taking it in turns to doze in the boat.

They passed the moored boats of Prosper's village at dawn and carried on until noon to a point where Malika said they were closest to her village. There they pulled the boat up on to the bank and made their way back on foot, Thomas stumbling along behind them in a torpid daze. *Like a plat eye*, thought Lizzie, before pushing the cruel idea from her mind.

The first sign of the village was the smell of wood smoke, mingling with roasting meat. As soon as they saw a thatched roof through a knot of vines they stopped. Lizzie recognised it as Malika's family home. Malika *and Zuri's* family home. She turned to Malika.

'Are you OK?' she said.

The girl nodded.

'Sure?'

Taking a deep breath, her hand on her mouth, Malika walked out of the jungle and immediately froze, spotting her mother sitting outside the house, talking to another woman as they ate their lunch.

It was Abena's companion who noticed Malika first, with the two white children standing behind her. She stood up shouting, lifting Abena with her and pointing.

Abena stood, looking into the eyes of her daughter, first with joy, then hope, and then a tremulous questioning.

And then with despair.

Chapter 25: Over the Pond

When she stepped out of the tirtha back into the garden, Lizzie found that Thomas was on his knees beside the mask, weeping into the long grass.

'We're back, back...' he was saying. 'Oh, *Mum*...'

'Yes, come on, quick,' she said, pulling him to his feet.

'Take me home!' he said.

'Yes, of course,' she said.

'No one is ever going to believe this,' he said.

Lizzie stared at the cut on his head, the redness of his sunburn, his lank, greasy hair, his torn and muddy T-shirt and shorts.

'You're right,' she said, realising then what she had to do.

'Come on,' she said, 'this way.'

She led him out of the garden and turned quickly down one of the hedged corridors.

'This place is a warren!' said Thomas as he followed her. She could sense his confidence returning rapidly.

'Did you hear that?' she said, stopping still.

'What?' He grabbed hold of her arm, looking around in panic.

'Someone's coming! We can't take any chances – it might be the demon!'

'No! What… what shall we do?'

'This way!' Lizzie ran to a turning in the corridor, pulling Thomas along behind her. They came to a gate and she led him through into a bright, sunlit garden with doll-like oriental houses, bonsai trees, a pond and a small yellow rock.

'I didn't hear anything,' said Thomas.

'We have to keep safe – if the demon comes back we're done for!' said Lizzie. 'Look – jump over that pond on to the yellow rock...'

He looked at her uncertainly. 'Why?'

'We need to get out of here, just until whoever it was has gone – trust me!'

'But...'

'Thomas – I've just travelled for nearly a week across the jungle to free you from a band of bloodthirsty killers – you've got to trust me now!'

'OK,' he said.

He stepped tentatively forward across the small pond – and disappeared.

*

Following him through the tirtha, Lizzie found him crouched on the ground, arms gripped around his sides, once again convulsed with fear. She looked along the still brown pool, surrounded by large rocks, with delicate bridges and a pagoda a short distance ahead.

'Come on, Thomas, come with me! There's someone here who can keep us safe from her, he has special powers.'

'Special powers?' muttered Thomas.

As she pulled the bewildered boy along by the wrist she thought about the outlandish images of baby demons and dragons and sword-wielding warriors that would still be swirling around his head after the transportation, and wondered whether he would crack before she even got to instigate her plan.

She just had to hope not.

She drew him along the path, past the trees that partially screened a view across a mighty broken valley with mountains all around, down over one of the bridges, through the pagoda, and on through more trees until they suddenly came up against a long terracotta wall with a single arched door.

'Where are we?' said Thomas.

'Don't think about it,' said Lizzie, opening the door and taking him through into the room beyond – a dark antechamber filled with sweet-smelling smoke, which led into a larger room with cushions on the floor and small pillars holding burning incense sticks. A single window lit up the dusty wooden interior, with its beautiful paintings of golden men and intricate coloured grids on the walls.

Sitting cross-legged on a cushion was a very old Chinese man in a saffron robe. His eyes were closed and he was chanting softly to himself:

'*Om mani padme hum...*'

Lizzie coughed and the man opened his eyes and looked up.

'Lizzie!'

'Who is that?' said Thomas.

'He's a monk, he'll help us. Thomas – you stay right here in this room, I just need to speak to him alone for a moment,' said Lizzie. She reached out to take the man's hand as he climbed to his feet.

'Don't leave me!' shouted Thomas, snatching hold of her T-shirt.

'Thomas! This is the last time I'll ask you to trust me, I promise!' Seeing the blind panic in his eyes, she added: 'Look, I know how scared you are. But I know all about this stuff, I've been going through these portals for nearly a year now. I know what I'm doing.'

She prised his fingers off her and, forcing a smile in an attempt to reassure him, led the baffled-looking Xing out of another door.

She was pleased to see Thomas still there, squatting in a dark corner, when they returned a few minutes later.

'I thought you weren't coming back!' Thomas cried, jumping up and once again pushing himself up against her. Lizzie did her best not to show her increasing irritation with the boy.

'I said I would, didn't I?'

'Young man,' said Xing, moving forward and putting one hand around Thomas' shoulder whilst the other remained in his pocket. 'Lizzie has just given me a very short summary of everything you've been through. You truly are a remarkable spirit.'

Thomas looked at the old man as if he was from another planet, but allowed himself to be led back out of the monastery and into the gardens, checking over his shoulder regularly to make sure Lizzie was behind them.

'I too was a very young man when I first discovered the magic of the portals, and realised that the world was so much more than it seemed,' continued Xing as they came up and through the pagoda. 'I remember first discovering this young English woman with wonderful cheekbones and blonde hair striding through this very garden and thinking... *how on earth did she get here?*

'Well, of course it was Evelyn, Lizzie's great-great aunt, a remarkable lady, and after just one afternoon talking together she took me into her confidence and asked me if I would like to come back with her through the portal and help her build her magical garden.

'What an opportunity! How could I refuse?' he said, as they came over the bridge, and walked along the stony path to the small shrine with its statue of the Buddha which marked the portal.

'And thus began the most marvellous relationship of my life – until this one,' he said, turning round and nodding at Lizzie.

'Now,' he said, stopping Thomas just as they reached the statue. 'You must promise to put all this suffering out of your mind for a while. You need a rest. No more dwelling on demons!'

He smiled, and took his hand off Thomas' shoulder. The boy looked puzzled.

'Just take hold of the statue and turn to your right,' said Xing, smiling.

Thomas did, and once more vanished.

Lizzie turned briefly to her friend. 'Thank you!' she said.

'I'm very, very glad you're back safe and sound,' he said.

'So am I,' said Lizzie. 'It's been... *awful.*' She forced an image of Zuri's face from her mind, realising it would catapult her into despair. 'Thank you,' she said again.

'I will come and see you soon. Very soon,' said Xing.

'Yes, please, I'm going to need you.'

'Good luck with the rest of your plan.' Xing drew his hand out of his pocket, and held up a small, yellowish lump.

A tooth.

Lizzie smiled, and reached for the statue of the Buddha.

*

In the Master of the Nets garden, Thomas was standing in the sunshine, stroking his head. He turned around quickly when he heard movement behind him.

'You...' he said.

'Hello Thomas,' said Lizzie. 'Are you OK now?'

'Wha... My head is killing me.' His fingertips brushed over the scar on the top of his forehead.

'Do you remember what happened?'

'Um – no. I mean... I remember... coming over here... yesterday evening...'

Lizzie shook her head slowly. 'Not yesterday evening. It was last Sunday. Your head, let me look at it.'

She stepped closer and pulled his fringe back from his forehead, examining the scab closely. Then, before she could stop herself, she kissed him quickly on the mouth.

'You don't remember tripping and hitting your head on the rock? In the woods?'

'No...'

'But... you do remember... everything else? Us... running away together?' She looked up at him uncertainly.

He looked at her, and for a moment she saw his eyebrows raise with something... *hope*.

'Well no... I don't think...'

'Oh no,' she whispered, looking down, and hurt.

'No – don't worry. Yes, I sort of...*do*... Just – the knock, it must have made me forget... some things...'

'Which is why we've had to come back, you remember? It was all going so nicely, just us alone together, sleeping under the stars or in that cabin, then back here in the Tower... just us and nature – but then you fell and hurt yourself and we knew... we knew we had to come back. No matter what the consequences.'

'Consequences?'

'Yes, because we've run away. We'll be missing persons. The police will be involved. Everyone will know.'

'Oh my God. What will Mum and Dad say?'

'I don't know… *sweetheart*. I just don't know.'

And then she led him out of the garden back into the house, where they found her mum with a policewoman.

Chapter 26: On Hay Bluff

Over the next fortnight she didn't get a moment to reflect on her ordeal.

When she wasn't being interviewed by the police and their child psychologist, a dreadful, over-familiar woman with dyed blonde hair and cold grey eyes, she was having to deal with her mum's fever pitch questions as well as phone calls from her gran in Croydon. She tried to keep her story as simple as possible so that she didn't catch herself out. Yes, she'd always hoped but had only found out just how much Thomas was in love with her when he stole into her garden a week ago, like in *Romeo and Juliet*. Yes, she was madly in love with him too. Yes, for the first two nights he'd stayed secretly in the garden's Tower, but then it had been her idea that they should properly run away together. Why? *This was the bit that hurt, but it was the only way to make it real* – because she was having trouble with her mum's relationship with Godwin, so soon after her dad's tragic death. So it was she who persuaded Thomas to do it? Yes. Didn't she think about the consequences – about their parents' worrying, about all the people that would get involved with searching for them? No. And how did you survive?

Sleeping under the stars. What did you eat? Food taken from home, and bought in preparation from the Spar. How did they avoid the search party? They circled round the edge of the line and came back into the garden, where they stayed in the Tower for a couple more nights. And what was their long term plan? *Well...* With that one, she just played dumb.

Luckily no one thought to ask why she was wearing jeans in the middle of summer, so no one discovered all the scratches, leech scars and mozzy bites on her legs. And she told them – *truthfully, this time* – that the scratch on her head was from running into a sharp branch in the dark.

The first time she managed to get out of the house, taking Mr Tubs for a walk in the woods, she was scared witless by a reporter who jumped out from behind a tree with a camera. She turned and fled as the woman pleaded for *just one question*, whilst Tubs yapped furiously and gave her time to get away.

So she ended up sitting in front of the TV – steadfastly avoiding the news ever since she'd seen *that* terrible photo of herself with greasy hair in her old Pink Pony sweatshirt – with Mr Tubs sat on her lap and her mum shuffling around them, angry one moment then morose the next.

And she did her best to block everything out of her mind, the lies, deception, guilt, her ordeal in the jungle – and the loss.

Especially the loss.

*

With the start of September came a sudden burst of cold air, all the more surprising given how hot the summer had been. Lizzie knew Godwin was coming to see her mum, presumably to try and smooth over her frostiness about the fact he'd been away and uncontactable when she needed him most. Lizzie used the opportunity to see if her mum would let her go and see Ashlyn, given that she would be back at school soon.

'You think I'm going to let you out of the house after this?'

'Please, Mum. I've been stuck in here for days now.'

'Supposing you're lying to me, and planning to see Thomas again!'

No way! thought Lizzie, before saying: 'I'm not, Mum. I promise.' She showed her mum the text from Ashlyn inviting her out for a morning.

'Why don't you have any friends your own age? Like normal girls?' said her mum. 'The only people you ever seem to spend any time with are adults – and now Thomas.'

'She was Eric's closest friend,' said Lizzie. 'We get on.'

She could see the pique in her mum's face before she looked away. For a moment Lizzie remembered the slender image of Jane with her long hair, kissing her dad in the jungle. The false vision, summoned up by Eva to crush her spirits. But its memory made her feel a pang of what... pity? *Sympathy?* Of *something* for her mum.

She could feel the friction in the air whilst her mum considered the request. Lizzie imagined the guilt she must be feeling about Godwin, compounded by the pain she had about her husband's betrayal – or *perceived* betrayal – and the fact her daughter got on better with the local village 'witch' than her.

Wow! It would all need unpacking some time, Lizzie knew. *But not now.*

'OK.' Her mum nodded, and walked off.

A near-perfect pass of guilt from mother to daughter.

*

Ashlyn picked her up in her car – an old, cream Morris Minor, similar to the cars Lizzie had seen so often in Kashi – and drove her out of England across the Welsh border, and up to a car park on the side of the nearest mountain, Hay Bluff.

As they walked up the blustery hillside Lizzie finished telling Ashlyn about her ordeal in the jungle, Eva's return, and the death of Zuri. They ended up sitting on a crag looking out over the valley, the wind and the view helping to put some distance between her and the events in Africa.

Then, when she had finished, Ashlyn told her about Caroline and Miles.

'I saw her!' Lizzie exclaimed, tears welling in her eyes. 'What?'

'Caroline – she appeared to me in a vision, after the chimps had attacked us – she was there before me, like when I first saw her that night, out on the bayou...'

Lizzie put her hand across her forehead. 'She said something to me. About *them* being gone – she must have

222

been talking about herself and Miles. And then she said something else, about it being *me* they needed now.'

Ashlyn looked at her. 'There's something more I need to tell you. Let's walk some more.'

So they continued up the grassy hill with its rough patches of dark rushes, up towards the summit.

'I'm worried about who might have shot them,' said Ashlyn.

Lizzie wiped her eyes with her sleeves, mopping away the tears.

'Not someone we know?'

'Hector described a man who stayed with them overnight in Cypress House. Someone who'd got lost in a storm and knocked on the door. An Englishman with silver hair and glasses, wearing tweeds.'

Lizzie felt goosebumps. *'Godwin?'* she whispered, appalled.

Ashlyn glanced at her, as the wind whipped her auburn hair. 'It sounds like him.'

'What are we going to do?'

'Be very careful. Watch him like a hawk.'

'But – he's going out with Mum! He practically *lives* with us. What if he does something to her… or me?'

'Lizzie, I'm very worried, for both of you. But… we can't be sure it was him and I suspect… I think he might not have intended to kill them. I think he was just after the doll, one of the Artefacts.'

'But I can't live with a murderer in the house!'

'We don't *know* it's him. And he doesn't know we suspect him. We'll just have to keep an eye on him, watch to see if he does anything suspicious.'

'That is so... *unsatisfactory*,' said Lizzie, realising the scale of her understatement even as she said it.

'Lizzie – what more can we do now? *Everything* is unsatisfactory.'

'I don't know. But what if Eva survived the blows from the Nkisi, and the fall with Zuri? What if she's still alive, and back with Godwin, and now they have the Nkisi *and* Caroline's doll? What then?' She thought momentarily about the small wooden head she'd brought back from Easter Island. *Was that an Artefact?*

Ashlyn shook her head. 'I don't know. We just have to keep our eyes open. And Eva hasn't been seen in the village since Kashi. She wouldn't dare turn up here again.'

They walked in silence for a while, deep in their own thoughts. Then Ashlyn said:

'There's something else too. Not so sinister, but just as important.'

'What?'

'You know I said I'd look some more into your family history, after you told me about your strange experience in Louisiana?' said Ashlyn. 'Well, I've been to the library in Hereford, talked to some of the old folk in the village, and read some more of Eric's journals.

'It turns out that Evelyn wasn't the first owner of Rowan Cottage. It was a derelict woodman's cottage, bought by a wealthy Quaker merchant, Bernhard Day, and his young wife, Hattie. They were Evelyn's parents, and they cleared the grounds and started laying out the garden.'

'So they were Eric's grandparents?' said Lizzie.

'Yes, that's right. Anyway, nothing strange in that. But then I spoke to a second cousin of Madeline's, a hundred-and-one-year-old lady in a home in Ledbury, who says her mother remembered the rumours about Hattie Swift, as she was first known.'

'What were the rumours?' said Lizzie, the intrigue and the wide open space temporarily lifting her spirits.

'I'll get to that in a bit. The woman, whose name is Nancy, said that Hattie was a headstrong young woman, with long dark hair, who first appeared in the village dishevelled and confused in a mighty storm. She was taken in and looked after by Bernhard, who ignored all the nasty gossip about her being a witch.

'Eventually they got married and bought the old cottage – on Hattie's request – and began to do it up. And then they had their children, Evelyn, Charles, and Mary, who was Eric's mother.'

'Still not so strange,' said Lizzie.

'No, but here's the odd bit. There's a long-running rumour amongst the Hebley Wiccans that our special abilities – the familiars, the power to do healing spells – is tied in with this *place*, and goes back to distant ancestors who were... well, to use a Christian phrase... *begotten, not created.* They weren't of the Earth, but came instead from a magical place.'

'The tirthas?' said Lizzie.

'Now that we know about the tirthas, it makes sense,' said Ashlyn. 'Now, Nancy later began to work for the registry office in Hereford and ended up filing old copies of marriage certificates. She came across Bernhard and Hattie's, and was intrigued by the names of Hattie's parents.'

'Which were?'

'James Swift and Isabella Jennings.'

'Nice names.'

'Yes,' said Ashlyn. 'But they were made up.'

'Hey?'

'At least that's what Nancy concluded, after searching all the local registers and speaking to lots of people. James' occupation was listed as a Hebley farmer, but there were no farmers in the area of that name.'

'Could just be a mistake,' said Lizzie.

'Yes, but then Nancy found Bernhard's closest friend, another Quaker called Peter Aldridge. Peter said that Bernhard had told him Hattie didn't know her parents, and had made the names up.'

'Why would she do that?'

'Well, Nancy – who's a Wiccan too – believes Hattie was an Arch Witch, *begotten not created*. And that when she turned up at Hebley on that first night, that was her first night *on the Earth*.'

Lizzie stopped, torn between amazement and disbelief.

'That would mean – let's get this right... oh no, I've no idea what she'd be... but it would mean that one of *my* relatives was an Arch Witch!'

'That's right,' said Ashlyn.

'You don't really believe that, do you?' said Lizzie.

'Why not?'

'Well...' They carried on climbing, heading along a thin black track made by sheep, whilst Lizzie thought about it.

'Do you think that's why I had that strange experience, then? When Pandu saw me in the garden?'

'Yes.'

'Wow. I mean – *wow*.'

Related to a witch. Someone who wasn't really born. *Get your head round that, Jones.*

'So – and I'm not saying I necessarily believe all this – but what you're saying is that Hattie came out of one of the garden tirthas as a kind of magical creature herself?' she said. 'Like *Eva?*'

'Yes, I'm starting to think it's possible,' said Ashlyn. 'Though she was good, not like Eva.'

'So my own *great-grand-whatever* actually first appeared on Earth after coming out of what was to become my garden?'

'Maybe.'

They walked on again in silence for a while, as they approached the brow of the mountain with its sweeping views over the town of Hay and the snaking River Wye. Lizzie spotted a few wild ponies, wandering along the brooding skyline.

'Hold on,' said Lizzie. 'Maybe that's what Caroline meant, about them being gone and it being *me* they need now. Maybe *they* need someone with Arch Witch ancestry, and I'm one of the few ones remaining. At least with a close witchy relative?'

'Well, I don't know,' said Ashlyn. 'But let's hope they – whoever *they* are, besides Eva, Paterson, and Lamya – are history now.'

'Yes,' said Lizzie, shuddering. 'Let's hope.' She couldn't imagine that whatever they wanted Caroline for could be anything pleasant.

When they reached the summit of the broad hill the wind began to blow hard. Lizzie looked out across the shaded ridges of the Black Mountains, folding into the distance. Bruised grey clouds raced across the sky.

Stark beauty, out of this world.

She felt Ashlyn's arm around her shoulders, as she began to cry.

Thank you for reading this book. If you enjoyed it, please consider telling your friends or leaving a review. Word of mouth is an author's best friend and much appreciated.

Other books in *The Secret of the Tirthas* series:

The City of Light
The Book of Life
The Lady in the Moon Moth Mask
The Unknown Realms

Also available

The Boy in the Burgundy Hood – *a ghost story*

Poetry

Up in the Air

Lizzie's adventures continue in…

The Lady in the Moon Moth Mask

She appears briefly, every third night, alone on The Edwardian Path.

A shimmering vision in white, whose only act is to slowly turn her hidden face up to Lizzie's window.

The Lady in the Moon Moth Mask.

Lizzie Jones is drawn by the mysterious Lady in the Moon Moth Mask back into the tirthas, the magical portals in her garden, to find an Artefact of Power, hidden in a different place and time.

But others are pursuing the lost Artefact – creatures of unspeakable evil who will do anything to avoid their summons to the terrifying place known as the Unknown Realms.

Can Lizzie and her friends stop the demons before a new evil comes into the world?

About the Author

I grew up in Warwickshire and worked for youth and environmental organisations in Wales and London. I now live in the Surrey Hills with my wife and two sons.

I've published poetry in magazines including *Poetry Ireland* and *Poetry Scotland*, and a poetry book, *Up in the Air*. My ghost story for adults, *The Boy in the Burgundy Hood*, was released in November 2019.

The Secret of the Tirthas was inspired by trips to India, Africa, and the US, as well as a real 'garden of rooms' deep in the English countryside.

If you want to be the first to hear about new books, you can subscribe to my mailing list by contacting me at stevegriffin40@outlook.com

To find out more and see photos of the places that inspired *The Secret of the Tirthas*, check out my website at steve-griffin.com. You can also connect with me on Facebook and Instagram using my handle @stevegriffin.author.